Praise for *Sacred City*

"*Sacred City* is a brilliant powerhouse that hit me like a poetry jam session, some damn fine urban-Indian music; Chicago honor song, love song, protest hymn, and dirge. Smart and smart-ass conversation, showing our slide from one cultural lexicon to another, all woven together in a Chi-Town Native special. *Sacred City* tells us real stories of people we might not know, but should. It maps layers of a sprawling town's history and its deep Indigenous roots. A dazzling achievement!"—SUSAN POWER, author of *Sacred Wilderness*

"Reading this one, you think *Sacred Smokes* never went over, but then you look down at this sidewalk Theo Van Alst's been leading you down and realize you're standing in *Sacred City*, and you kind of never want to leave, so long as he'll keep telling these stories."—STEPHEN GRAHAM JONES, author of *The Only Good Indians*

"Tecumseh said, 'The Great Spirit above knows no boundaries,' and neither does Ted Van Alst: the stories in *Sacred City* are electrifying, propulsive, and light up the land with indignation and fierce compassion. Here are stories about people's struggles that are as heartbreaking and gritty as they are ingenious. I loved it."—BRANDON HOBSON, National Book Award finalist and author of *The Removed: A Novel*

"*Sacred City*'s swagger is as sacred as it is profane. Van Alst's writing is ancient blood screaming through the streets of Chicago. This is more than literature; it's history, love, violence, ancestral knowledge, and brotherhood thrown on the page with the power of a Molotov cocktail and the precision of a lyricist. I'd say something about transcendence and the universe, but this book taught me not to think so small."—GABINO IGLESIAS, author of *Coyote Songs*

"Van Alst's writing is riveting and funny as hell; brutal, blunt, and utterly unique YA. *Sacred City* is a serious ass kicking—a young-adult voice with poetry and violence and a history that feels too present day to call prescient overflowing its pages. I cannot recommend strongly enough, and as with Van Alst's previous work, I wish I was still teaching high school language arts, because *Sacred City* certainly belongs on the syllabus."—KIMBERLY DAVIS BASSO, author of *I'm a Little Brain Dead* and *Birth and Other Surprises*

"In this collection of vivid, visceral, and vital stories, Theodore C. Van Alst Jr. reminds us that Native American voices cannot be contained."—BILL SAVAGE, Northwestern University

SACRED CITY

SACRED CITY

Theodore C. Van Alst Jr.

University of New Mexico Press | Albuquerque

ISBN 978-0-8263-6286-5 (paper)
ISBN 978-0-8264-6287-2 (electronic)

Library of Congress Cataloging-in-Publication Data is on file with the Library of Congress.

Founded in 1889, the University of New Mexico sits on the traditional homelands of the Pueblo of Sandia. The original peoples of New Mexico—Pueblo, Navajo, and Apache—since time immemorial have deep connections to the land and have made significant contributions to the broader community statewide. We honor the land itself and those who remain stewards of this land throughout the generations and also acknowledge our committed relationship to Indigenous peoples. We gratefully recognize our history.

Cover illustration: *Power of the Tongue*. Acrylic. 18 × 24. 2019.
"As a young kid growing up on Cut Bank Creek, I always enjoyed wild stories, and that of course led to a wild imagination. Especially stories from here, and those stories allowed me to imagine beings. Sort of like Napi and Coyote, free to make their choices. Some were good, some were bad, and some were in-between. Lately I've been noticing how often the reservation life is fraught with lateral violence, jealousy, and gossip. Which it's always been (at least if you were a smart kid and grew up with a different way of looking at things). Which made me think of the power of the tongue, something my grandfather always talked to me about as a boy. It has the power to bring life or death, and there's a lot of tricksters out there walking around with that power."—Lauren Monroe Jr.
Designed by Felicia Cedillos
Composed in ScalaOT 10.25/14

As always, for Amie, Emily, and Max

Contents

To all of the Indians who will not be ghosts.

Credits

Some of the stories published here originally appeared in the following publications:

> *The Journal of Working-Class Studies*: "By the Slice"
> *Literary Orphans*: "Boy Joe"
> *Mad Scientist Journal*: "Afterworlds" (published as "Guts")
> *Massachusetts Review*: "The Boys are Back in Town"
> *Open: Journal of Arts & Letters*: "Test Pattern"
> *Red Earth Review*: "Where's the Sunshine?" (published as "Sunshine")
> *Red Ink: International Journal of Indigenous Literature, Art & Humanities*: "Coyote Drinks"
> *Unnerving Magazine*: "The Lamb" (published as "Sacrifices")
> *Yellow Medicine Review*: "Cedar" and "Up Yours, Tom Wolfe" (published as "A Man Not Full, or Fuck You, Tom Wolfe")

Support literary journals and magazines!

Sihasapas Blackfeet. Haunts and homes same as the Unkpapas; number, 165 lodges. These two bands have very little respect for the power of the whites. Many of the depredations along the Platte are committed by the Unkpapas and Sihasapas, whose homes are farther from it than those of any other of the Titonwans.

—GEN. G. K. WARREN, 1856

Distinctly against the spirit of their treaties, the council turned to consider intertribal relations. Since their brief truce with the Crows had broken down in 1853, Hunkpapa and Sihasapa war parties had infested the lower Yellowstone valley, waging open war on the River Crows, which they categorically refused to give up.

—KINGSLEY M. BRAY, *CRAZY HORSE: A LAKOTA LIFE*

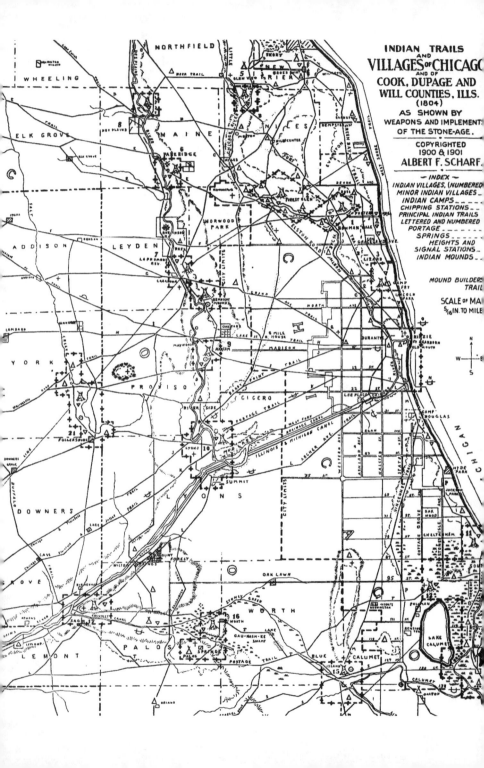

INDIAN TRAILS
AND
VILLAGES OF CHICAGO
AND OF
COOK, DUPAGE AND
WILL COUNTIES, ILLS.
(1804)
AS SHOWN BY
WEAPONS AND IMPLEMENTS
OF THE STONE-AGE.

COPYRIGHTED
1900 & 1901
ALBERT F. SCHARF.

— INDEX —
INDIAN VILLAGES, (NUMBERED)
MINOR INDIAN VILLAGES
INDIAN CAMPS
CHIPPING STATIONS
PRINCIPAL INDIAN TRAILS
LETTERED AND NUMBERED
PORTAGE
SPRINGS
HEIGHTS AND
SIGNAL STATIONS
INDIAN MOUNDS

MOUND BUILDERS
TRAIL

SCALE OF MAP
5/16 IN. TO MILE

(Opposite page)

"Indian Trails and Villages of Chicago and of Cook, Dupage, and Will Counties, Ills. (1804) as shown by weapons and implements of the stone age." Albert F. Scharf / Public domain.

We lived in apartments on Birchwood and then on Chase. I spent a big chunk of my life as a kid in the Indian Boundary lands north of the old treaty line that made it illegal for Native folks to be anywhere inside most of Chicago back in the day. The boundary line is from the first angled line above Devon all the way down to Lake Calumet, and you know I crossed over every chance I got, even if I didn't think about it each time. Well, not every single time, I suppose, but just about; Rogers Avenue ran right through the middle of my every day. This map shows the terrain of the people below the city—Chicago is an overlay on Native land and stories that seep and burn through all the cracks every chance they get.

As many have known and Dorene Wiese has said, "Chicago has always been Indian Country."

The whites have books, many books. And in those books they tell of the Indians—and what the white man writes, the white man reads and believes. I have read many stories of the fight in Chicago, and they all speak of the deviltry and the treachery of the Indians. I am writing a book that will tell of the treachery of the white man. I will tell the truth as my father told it to me when he was middle-aged and when he was old and dying, and all the time the tale was unchanged in the telling. Some men and a woman—whites, all of them—have written stories of the fight between the soldiers and the Potawatomi. Now let an Indian tell it.

—SIMON POKAGON

O-o-h child
Things are gonna get easier
O-o-h child
Things'll get brighter

—THE FIVE STAIRSTEPS

1. THE BOYS ARE BACK IN TOWN

This land is our land, and not yours.

—CONFEDERATED TRIBES, 1752

After a brief sojourn to sunny California and the sunnier southwest, I return to my homelands.

They welcome me with that incomparable Chicago humidity, wet saran wrap clinging to your face wrapped in a smoke-soaked pillowcase. Breathing, like sliding out of trouble, is laborious. But it's my reservation, and there's no place I'd rather be, even in the summer.

Cause summertime in this here city means the balls on Sheridan's horse will be painted bright-cherry red, we'll be selling bags of lukewarm Old Style tallboys at ChicagoFest to tourists from the burbs while we show them the frosty ones in our Styrofoam cooler of ice, means the alley vomit dries quicker even if it stinks worse while it does, and how except for flies, we don't really have bugs, unless you're hanging in the woods by the Northwestern tracks or out in the forest preserves, home of powwows and sick aluminum bat fights with Gaylords at ten thousand baseball diamonds. Oh yeah.

Summer.

Mars lights blue and red popping piss everywhere gunshots screams wind and ozone weak warm rain that never washes anything away tavern smells liquor cigarettes pizza baking everywhere ting ting ting of helado man running from the cops laughing drinking browner by the day.

SpanishEnglishPolishSerbianCreoleMandarinJamaican GermanArabicArmenianJapaneseRussianIrishSwedishBengali TobaganYiddishIndianHillbillyHindiBajanNorwegianCroat FrenchUkranianAlbanianItalianUrduAssyrianBlackWhite YellowRedBrownsparklingmidnightbrightdayrainorshinethese wordseverywherethisisRogersFuckingPark, y'all.

It feels real. Like when this one time . . .

I'm feeling poppin' fresh my damn self, cause my girlfriend just hickied me a three-pointed cross that runs from the middle of my chest down to the top of my belly button. We're drinking in the middle of the day, cause we can. We're sitting on the farthest bench in Pottawattomie Park, the one at the north end, just off Fargo, across from the community garden and looking out on the athletic fields. The sky is burnt silver and it smells like it wants to rain, but we know it won't. We'll just sweat here and wait for something to happen. We've got about forty icy-ass-but-warming-fast Old Style brown glass keg bottles in paper bags in the bushes and a brick of Richard's Wild Irish Rose, fresh batteries in the boombox, and all the girls are there, which means we're stuck listening to whatever they like, Commodores or Diana Ross or Kool and the Gang or some shit. We'll see how long that lasts once we start getting drunk.

So we're just chilling in the park. Nothing much going on, we talk shit, make fun of each other, the usual. Everyone's hanging out:

JD (run that J and that D together, say it "jayyyde") sits on the top slats on the bench next to me, trots his leg like he just did something bad or is thinking about something worse; all the Jimmys; everyone's girlfriends. Even Freckles is there, the ginger hillbilly fuck. Dude never really looked quite right, you know? I mean, shit, his skin was Band-Aid colored. What the hell is that? I relax, read a little. When it comes to books I want to be buried with one open over my face, like I fell asleep reading and it just plopped there. Got this new one from Jackie Collins, probably *Chances*. It had that fine-ass Lucky Santangelo in it, anyway. I study the dialogue. I love that shit, and Jackie is the best. I need to take my mind off stuff. Late yesterday sucked. Dark fuckin night, man. I was feeling desperate. I tried to sell my soul to the devil, and he just leaned in close and laughed. Put his Lucky Strike out on the back of my hand and walked through my bedroom door. Fuck that guy.

I look up and see Montell heading our way from Rogers Ave. His nickname is Bubba. He doesn't like that, but it is what it is. Anyways, as you can imagine from the name, he doesn't move too fast. I chug the rest of my beer as I watch him make his way across the baseball diamond and then the grass. I open another and light a smoke. He's still coming when I finish the bottle and reach for a replacement. I'm halfway through that one when finally

"What up, Teddy?"

"You see it, brother."

"Cool, cool. What's up Folks?" he makes the rounds with everyone, shakes hands sideways, dropping the crown, teaching them all the different ways to shake hands like Royals.

Montell is a Farwell and Clark Royal. I'm originally from Touhy and Ridge, the branch that had members who would eventually make up the core of his branch. I'm a few years older than him. I've been a warlord, a vice-president, and a president of the Pee Wee set. Most sets of Simon City Royals back then had Futures,

3

Pee-Wees, Juniors, then Seniors. I still hold it down for T/R, my original set, cause that's what you fuckin do, at least the way I was taught.

"When you gonna go F/C, Teddy?"

"Never, Montell. You know that," I laugh.

"C'mon man. Stop fucking around." His eyebrows tense.

"We'll see, Folks," I say.

"What about these motherfuckers?" he says, hands thrown wide, face relaxed.

"Cain't say, homes," I say. "They needa get initiated in."

"Well let's do it," he smiles.

"They're chickenshits," I say.

"Fuck that," Freckles pops off. "I was a Pope. I was jumped in at—"

"Man, be quiet," me and Montell both say.

I have one of those times where you decide to do something, you know, the ones where you're out of your body watching and going what the fuck is coming out of my mouth right now.

I say, "Let's do this, Montell. Let's show 'em how it's done."

While experiencing my astral projection moment it occurs to me that this is actually a really bad idea. Two or three days ago I got into it with Chupe down by the Howard Street El. We go to school together, and since there's me and all the other Royals have dropped out it's really just me (but see that story I told you about Lord Black and the CVLs from before; no serious worries) so I sometimes have to listen to his shit because there's an assload of Kings from multiple branches there, but now it's summer and all bets are off so fuck him. We humbugged for a bit. I tagged him in the face a couple of times but he got a nice shot in on my ribs and I heard a little crack so score for Chupe but man that shit hurts and I'm aware that this could be a problem but I'm a little bit drunk with a whole lot to prove, who knew? I decide to demonstrate a simple initiation.

It goes like this nowadays. You face one guy, bend forward, and he leans down, full nelsons you, wraps up your arms and whatnot, and everybody else pounds the living shit out of you, feet, fists, elbows, whatever, until the first guy calls it, tells them to stop. Usually if your face isn't buried in his gut enough blood runs out onto the ground under you and they can see it's probably time to stop. Make sure you don't yell or holler too much, cause that'll just make them mad. It gets a little Jack and Piggy sometimes.

———

Montell handles the initiation. I'm trying to teach these guys something. Remember, my girlfriend had just hickied that three-pointed cross on me and I gotta represent. They give it to me good, but not that good, cause none of them have been initiated before, got no real sense of vengeance or pain. When I got jumped in as a Future it was in Kid's basement. I was eleven turning twelve and walked into a blacked-out room where Twat promptly round-housed me in the face. That was his signature move. I knew it was coming, but, pitch-black room, so I never saw it. About ten juniors were beating the shit out of me so bad Kid had to fall on me, tell me to protect my nuts and took three or four shots to his own head that were meant for my face. I got a little break in the nose, lots of blood, one hell of a shiner, the title of Warlord over the protests of Kid's own brother *and* a walk home with the hottest girl in the set. Sometimes it pays to just shut up and take it.

This time ain't shit compared to that. Except someone found those ribs. Fuck, man. Bubba. Tie this shirt around my chest. It's a dago tee, so there's not much material. Shit. I step on the bottom edge and pull up on the straps, stretch it out. I hand it to him. Cicadas drone and I think I see twists of steam above the grass out in the soccer field. Someone cuts off the third-in-a-row play of Paul

Revere's Ride and I pull the shirt sideways across my chest, give Montell the two loose ends.

"Not too—"

He yanks the leads together, his knee in the middle of my back.

"hard," I say.

He pulls a little tighter

and I hear bone ends grind.

My left eye waters, the line of nerve and muscle just below the skin of my face pulling diagonally down my body to my right side. I feel a click as he ties the ends together. Damnit. Half my cross is covered up now. It's kinda funny, but does it hurt? Only when I breathe. Forget about laughing for a month.

The endorphins are great, though. I'm high as a kite. Way better than when you're getting fucked up and you smack your head against the brick so you can get that little bit of your body's own opiate production. The external catalyst is always better, comes with a bigger rush. And right now, my brain's trying to OD me on its own shit.

We cut the music back on and it's Judas Priest and Sugarhill Gang and then Triumph, but we booted that shit. We knew even then they sucked, and years later I'd boo them at an Iron Maiden concert for talking shit about devil worship. Not because I gave a shit about devil worship or was even a Christian but because no one ever took up for Lucifer. And after all, as Saul Alinksy said, we really should pour one out every now and again for the first guy to rise up and successfully demand his own kingdom.

I perch on the top slat of the bench. It's one of those ones that sits on rough concrete legs with three wide planks up the back painted brown and one long plank for a seat. Fine urban design. I tap my foot on the seat part, ratty-ass black Converse hi-tops with wide royal-blue b-boy laces.

Bubba walks over, laughs, shakes his head.

"Damn, Midget. Ya lookin rough, brotha. I think you're scaring these boys."

I say "hahaha" but don't laugh, cause ribs.

"You gonna let us have them?"

"You mean for Farwell?" I say.

"Yeah," he smiles. Montell has one of those voices where he always sounds like he has a chest cold or something. It makes him sound emotional, but he ain't.

"Shiiit," I say. "They ain't mine. I ain't trying to start no set. I just like chilling over here at the park."

"We'd still hang here sometimes," he tells me.

"I'll *always* hang here," I tell him. "This is Pott-a-fuckin-watt-o-mie Park, bro."

"You ain't coming with us, Teddy?"

"I tol' you man. I'll think about. Now drink with me, brotha," I say, trying to deflect.

"Alright, Midget," he says. Hands me a beer. "You know what?" he says.

"What, motherfucker? Why you looking at me like that?"

Then he tells me, now he tells me. Tiger and the rest of those crowns from Howard Street are fixin to move on us. He heard it from one of the Columbia and Ashland Kings' sister who works in the new place called Taco Bell. But I was worried a little. You know how the first time you get the breath knocked out of you and you think you're going to die? Somewhere between that and the first time you're in your twenties doing coke and you finally get a chest pain you're sure is a heart attack? In between there is the itchiness of realizing your own mortality. It doesn't bug you enough that it's consuming, but it's when you start making little deals with Creator so you don't unexpectedly die doing something really stupid.

I take too big a drag off a smoke and when I cough, the edge of one of my ribs reminds me how vulnerable I am right now. I look around me though, and I feel okay. I look at my boys and our girls and I know that we are far less a lost than a deserted generation. But we're on this fuckin island together and yeah we're gonna be okay. We celebrate that fact for a while.

The wood on the bench just to my left frags out and splinters pop up in slow motion and I can see a curl of smoke behind where a bullet's dug its way into the wood about two inches from my leg and the pop registers in my head. Motherfucker.

Tiger's here.

I look up and over across the community gardens. Tiger, Taco Jr., and a couple of their white boys are moving our way quicklike. Tiger's fucking with the slide on some automatic piece of shit he probably found in a dumpster hahaha jammed I think fuck you and Taco Jr. is looking over the top of a revolver. This prick is the most Indian looking dude I know, but there ain't no brotherhood here. Goddamnit I hate this sonofabitch.

"JD! You strapped?"

"No," he kinda mumbles.

"What? You always got something."

"Cops took it this morning." He shakes his head to flick that mass of greasy hair out of his eyes.

Shit.

Freckles pulls out a .25.

"Gimme that." I grab the piece.

I turn and pop off a couple of shots at Taco Jr.

The windshield in a 1980 baby-blue Regal collapses. The other hits something that makes it make that *whhhiiirnnng* sound like in the Westerns.

The Coronas duck behind the line of parked cars.

"RUN YOU MOTHERFUCKERS," I yell at everyone.

This .25 is a regular shorty clip, so I only got four shots left.

The girls grab the boombox and two of the Jimmys grab up the beer. I appreciate their sense of priority, remind myself to thank them later. "Pinche cabrón!" I yell. "Chinga tu madre bitch!" My next shot takes out a headlight. I see Taco Jr.'s long black hair blow back from around the edge of the hood he's crouched next to. Just missed. Tiger still ain't got his piece of shit figured out, so it's me against Taco Jr. and a dusty-ass revolver he probably got from Pancho Villa's stash.

I hop-walk backward kinda quicklike, two hands on the .25 extended out in front of me. The Kings're still hiding behind the cars. I sneak a look over my shoulder, see Montell herding the crew toward the field house about 150 yards away. When I turn my eyes back in front, I see one of the white boys stand up next to a black Caprice. Pop! I take out its windshield. The sight on this thing sucks. Fuck, I think. Somebody's gonna be busy with the glass jobs later. He ducks back down. I'm already halfway to the building and these Kings are fading fast. Right when I think we're clear though, Tiger figures out his jam and *poppoppop* three shots whiz by. I don't hear anybody yell, so all clear. I'm still moving quicklike and I yell out Royal Love! King Killer! Queen Thriller! and turn and make the corner toward the tennis courts. For some reason I think of how we catch bumblebees in the morning glories that cover the chain link that fences everything in, how we pinch the ends shut while the bees are busy, shake the shit out of them trapped in the petals then set the bees free into the trash can where they promptly take it out on one of those fucking yellow jackets. I look over my shoulder and see them standing around in the street, yelling and talking shit to each other. I know they won't come all the way in here, so I relax. The .25 is too hot to stick down my pants so I shove it in my back pocket. I creep back to the edge of the fence and watch them walk away, arms waving around as crappy Spanish and worse English swear words drift my way and I laugh a little, light a smoke. I get to the tennis courts and lean back into the pale-blue morning glories, tilt my head up, close my eyes, and

then I'm like one of those kites you can buy at Open Pantry for seventy-nine cents, the ones you put together made of paper and pine dowels, I'm a vulture with two big yellow eyes and purple-black wings that drifts up on this warm eyewatering wind and watches down on it all happening to us.

It's still only all I can do.

2. SIMON CITY

I have made diligent inquiries of the headmen of different tribes as to what estimate they place on the half-breeds among them. Their general reply has been, 'They are certainly an improvement on the pale face, but not on the red man.' . . . Yet, notwithstanding such an unfortunate mixture, we find some grand characters who have been able to rise high above the sins of parentage.

—SIMON POKAGON, "THE FUTURE OF THE RED MAN"

Those rocks, those slabs? We own them. Even as the water will swallow them whole.

"What do you mean, grandfather?"

I mean what I say. We own them and all of this beach as far as we can see. The Bodéwadmik, the Potawatomi, yes, but now I suppose, all the Mis-ko-au-ne-ne-og', the red men. This is our land.

We're walking toward the breakwater at Jarvis Beach. I have a look up and down the sand, lean out over the concrete and granite, see the piers sticking out in the water, red beacons on their rusty tower ends lighting up the night and the flat surface of Lake

Michigan. My eyes travel south, over field houses and hotdog and tamale stands, pick up the big lights at Montrose and Belmont Points. Shit, even though the air around us is fuzzy, it's so clear down that way I think I can make out the yachts in Monroe Harbor.

My brain's a little foggy here, too, but I don't really remember what he's talking about.

"How's that?" I tilt my head, look in his face.

Do you know how to read? He doesn't return the gaze.

"I do."

They still don't teach our history, do they? We talk about it sometimes. Well, mostly I do, but the old men listen on occasion. We thought maybe after all this time they'd run out of things to talk about, might talk about our things. So, you don't know about the Sand Bar Claim?

"I do not."

When the whites made their treaty with us to steal Chicago away, they asked for all the land available at the time. But they neglected to cover the lake bottom or any "made land" in their paper. Our grandfathers figured in their greed the whites would run out of land and they were right. All of these railroads and piers and parks are built on new land they had to create. None of that new land was covered under the original treaty, so we own it still.

My head wraps around this and I smile, big.

"So, all this is still yours, ours?"

That's right, grandson.

"How do we get it back?"

I made the claim for it. Went all the way to their Supreme Court.

"No shit? Whoops. Sorry." I put my hand over my face.

No, it's fine. We hear your generation's foul mouths. It's fine to use those words when necessary, but you seem to find them necessary all the time.

"Times have changed."

Touché, as the whites say.

We make our way down to the beach, walk awhile.

I stop by a pair of buckthorns wrestling over a little patch of green at the edge of the sand, light a cigarette. Offer one.

Machine-rolled? Thank you.

I flick my lighter again, cup my hands for him, the smoke rolling up from the cigarette clenched in my teeth straight into my face. I squint against the acrid wisps, eyes watering.

His eyes look up over the flame into mine, crinkle at the corners. He laughs, says,

What's wrong, grandson? Those are prayers to the Creator. Don't be so soft. Sometimes you need to suffer a little to make your voice heard.

"I'm fine." I hold back a cough.

He drags deeply, sends a huge grey plume skyward.

These are good.

He holds it out at arm's length, admiring it. Not bad. You take this and so many things for granted. We worry about you.

"We know you tried for us. Tried so hard. I'm not sure we're doing all we can."

We can see all that's happened. Their wars. Their armies are bigger every day.

"Resistance is almost impossible. They destroy whole worlds at a time now."

That's true, grandson. But there've been moments.

"Like Wounded Knee?" I flick my ash.

Yes. Like Wounded Knee. We saw that one.

"Did you see the jet fighters and armored personnel carriers and automatic rifles?"

We did.

"Then you know."

We know the spirit was there, that Spirit was there.

"It's an army of empire. The most powerful the world has ever known."

The same empire met us when they were children. We fought them then. You can fight them now.

His smoke is burned halfway to the butt already. He looks at it, flicks the long ash off with a translucent finger, sighs.

"How, grandfather? They have no regard for life anymore. There's no parlay with them." I try not to sound spleeny, fail.

It's in their laws.

"But it's in their courts." Damnit. That tone again.

Facts and moral high ground. He squints out over the water.

"We may have the facts, but they have no morality," I say, with whatever authority teenagers might possess.

We finish our smokes, looking down the shore. The lights look back, unblinking.

He twists into the mist, leaving the same way he had come.

3. UNSETTLING

It is important for us, my brothers, that we exterminate from our lands this nation which seeks only to destroy us.

—PONTIAC

Writers are thieves who steal stories and pawn them on paper. I think about that under the graywashed sodium arc light as I carve an Old English-style 𝕾ℭℜℑℵ𝕾𝔊 nice and deep into the brown enamel–painted wooden Pottawattomie Park bench with my butterfly knife. Would someone ever steal this story? Translate what happened at its inscription, what they thought had happened, what they hope had happened? What would they say, what would they write? Would those be very different things, the spoken how of their transit to Simon City Royal / North Side Gangster territory, their "discovery" of these words and symbols, and their written account of their transgression and trespass into a world not theirs, though created by their mothers and fathers and left to us, places they'd rather not know about, at least until we had vacated them, silver-shoveled gentrifiers skulking in our wake to repackage and resell this twice-stolen land in Chicago to the daughters and sons of eternal pioneers, ceaseless settlers in a country that will ever unsettle and elude their alien souls?

That answer is going to have to wait, cause there's some alien souls trying to creep up on us right now from the back of 3-D, the third baseball diamond in the park. I take a big swig off this paper bag–wrapped quart of Old Style and check their progress out of the side of my eye from the tracks on down to the backstop behind home plate, about a hundred and fifty yards across the field between us. I count three Latin Kings and one Howard Street Lord. I think about him and wonder why his set ever united with these Corona motherfuckers. And then I remember they lost one of their boys to John Wayne Gacy. Prolly scared, I guess. Between creeper cops and suburban murderers, their shrinking membership needed all the help they could get.

We had shot out the big floodlights above the diamond at 3D a few days ago, and right now I'm glad I decided to chill at this end of the park and wait for Jimmy and JD and them to get back from a National's run. That's one of those runs you do at the grocery store where you fill the bottom of a shopping cart with beer, throw a bunch of tortillas and ham and cheese and chips and shit on top and roll that fucker right out the door to your buddies who are waiting to grab up everything and run like banshees across the parking lot and up the railroad tracks. The National's at Rogers and Clark was our local store. It was an A&P's and then eventually became an Aldi's. I think that was right after my brother snorted a bunch of tic and sledgehammered his way through the cinder-block wall next to the tracks so he could get some gum or whatever the hell he needed that night. Don't ask me why all the stores in Chicago get a possessive "s" when you say their name. They just do.

I didn't recognize any of the Kings at first, just knew that's what they were because of the direction they came from. Howard Street east of Ashland was their turf, so to get to us they'd either have to biddly bop up Rogers Avenue or come up Birchwood and then down Wolcott, but we'd see their asses all those ways, and taking the alley between Winchester and the gardens was suicide, cause all those families that lived along there were outside at night *and* on our side. So these were Kings. Plus that HSL.

As I set down my beer and reach over to turn down the NWA on the boombox a little and hope the fellas remembered to throw some batteries in the cart, I see Jimmy and JD out of the corner of my other eye making their way around the corner on the path from the field house over by Rogers. They've got two of the other Jimmys with them along with Freckles and—what?!—Bubba and Cesar from Farwell and Clark, and holy shit it looks like Lil Theo and a couple of Popes. There must've been a meeting or something. Yup. Probably, cause I can see Bubba holding his sawed-off shotgun down by his leg as he's walking. Dude is such a show-off. I love this guy.

But shit. They only have one big brown paper shopping bag. JD's holding it from the bottom while he pimps up the path. As they get closer, I hear bottles clanking. Cool. Beer at least.

I look over at them, do the head nod over to my left a couple times, toward the Kings who are halfway across the yellowed grass on the dry and brittle field. My set looks over, and now chock full of confidence, so do I. I see some long black hair. That's Taco Jr. along with Tiger and Chupe. I laugh to myself. Nice try, fuckers. They keep on coming. I don't think they've seen everyone yet.

JD and the crew are close enough that I can holler over to them.

"Hey, man. How come you only got one bag? That ain't enough beer for all of us."

Jade says, "We ain't got no beer. The manager took our cart."

"So what's in the bag?"

"You'll see," he says, and they start to hustle up a little bit.

The Kings are committed now, too close to turn and run. Taco Jr. reaches in his jock and pulls out a little chrome piece of shit, a .25 or a .32. I laugh as Bubba racks a shell in that Mossberg of his.

The set gets to the bench and I say,

"What the fuck's in the bag, man?"

JD holds it open for me, and I see a dozen Molotov cocktails ready to go.

We smile at each other just as Taco and Tiger come within throwing range.

4. THE BEACH

At the World's Fair on Chicago Day, after ringing the new Liberty Bell, and speaking in behalf of my people, I presented Mayor Harrison, according to the programme of the day, with a duplicate of the treaty by which my father, a Pottawattamie chief, in 1833, conveyed Chicago—embracing the fair-grounds and surrounding country—to the United States for about three cents per acre. In accepting the treaty, the venerable Mayor said: "grateful to the spirit of the past, I am happy to receive this gift from the hand of one who is able to bestow it. Chicago is proving that it recognizes the benefits conferred through this treaty. I receive this from an Indian all the more gratefully because in my own veins courses the blood of an Indian. Before the days of Pokagon, I had my origin in the blood that ran through Pocahontas. I stand to-day as a living witness that the Indian is worth something in this world.

—SIMON POKAGON, "THE FUTURE OF THE RED MAN"

"Leave the beer. That'll pay part of your asshole tax."

Waves crash and roar, green and grey on the shores of Lake Michigan on the North Side of Chicago. North Side, best side, land of my birth. There's no other place I'd rather be, and my bones tell me so. Warmth like morphine heat buzzes through my frame, throbs up through my skin, pops out and hugs my skinny ass and tells me it's going to be okay, while its gold light washes out over my wide eyes and death is so very far away.

Shitty, but not sloppy drunk, we weave through weathered benches and garbage-strewn dunes, closed hotdog shacks, and piles of Park District canoes, making our way south, a warm wind from the west running into the cold breeze off the lake in the purple-black sky right above us. There's no rain, but it feels like thunder pours down on our heads; long hair, curly hair, afros, and grown-out summer baldy-sours all bristle with the wild static in the air. Ball lightning flares out blue and white in silent pops over the dark horizon to the east, its orange echoes mocking my ears, waiting for the thunder that still never comes.

Growing up by the lake has affected me my whole life. If I don't live by, can't walk to or see big water, I feel it every day. Its lack makes me morose and mopey and maladjusted. The bones don't lie. I even come down here in the winter; the frozen waves on the breakers and the moaning of the ice along the shore speak to me in ways that give me place, tell me I'm home. On this late summer night, I'm happy to be alive, though I'm not sure if it's the beach or my set—my fam, or the post-fight buzz—but nights like this, it doesn't matter either way.

We're heading toward Farwell Pier. We can see shadows out there night fishing, lanterns and little bonfires built in hibachis and homemade grills lighting the black water and framing their bent bodies and old man fishing gear in a flickering yellow glow. Sometimes we trade beers, sometimes joints, for whatever they've caught and cooked. Usually perch, but sometimes coho, and smelt in the spring. We shoot the shit, learning old guy jokes and how we shouldn't fish with M-80s and nets, cause that ain't fair.

Tonight, we're generous, handing out weed and beers, full of our own jokes and glow, talking shit and sharing old stories. We're getting back from a humbug with some Latin Kings at Leone Beach, a serious threat to our extended territory, one we were fortuitously and fucking happy to have been at. Six Coronas and about fifteen of us Royals. We all like the water and the sand, going to the beach, so yeah, that worked out. It was kind of nice, this old school humbug. Folks was packing, but no one drew up. Just some straight ass-beating. Them's the breaks. No particular hate, just their bad timing. It's happened to us, and this time it happened to them.

So yeah, we were fired up, full of that youthful sauce that pulls up genuine smiles, true joy, love maybe even, that space created with your boys when you can imagine nothing really bad has happened, and everything really good is possible. Those maybe two moments you get growing up, the ones that slip past you before you have a chance to clock them for what they are. Those two moments would have to wait, though, because I was about to have one of those other kinds of moments.

"What?"
"Yeah. Just give us the beer and walk away," I say.

I had wandered away from the pier into one of the little dunes that sprung up around Pratt Ave. beach. I was thinking about taking a piss, and a few of the peewees had followed along behind me, anxious to keep talking, jostling for position, trying to one-up their warlord, thoughts of leadership dancing in their heads. I needed to take a leak, so I kept walking farther into the beach grass and scrubby buckthorns.

That's when I hear a group of guys talking about college or some shit.

I listen as I look for a place to piss, one ear vaguely cocked toward the peewees telling me how down they were for the Nation, and the other sifting through the college-boy yow.

After thirty seconds or so I realize I know these guys. I had gone to grammar school and then high school with them.

Or *been* at the same high school, since once we got there they didn't, wouldn't, talk to me, acted like they had never seen me in their life. And after I dropped out, well, whatever.

I walk out between a couple of bushes and there they are, a little anxiety ridden, glancing around, unsure if they should plant it there and party or not.

I keep that vibe going for them.

"Hey," I continue.

"Oh, wow. It's you," one of them says. Not sure which one, but who gives a fuck.

"Yeah. It's me. Not sure what you're doing here, but like I said, just leave the beer and we're good."

"What? We were—"

"—going to leave the beer," I finish for him.

"Come on, Teddy. It's not like that," he says.

"Oh, but it is," I say, looking around at the half-dozen assholes who had dried up out of my life, their faces even now turning to dust in front of my eyes.

Three and a half years or so run between us like a VHS on fast forward. I watch it play out on his face, his college-bound senses undulled for the moment, my ignored humanity lurching back into his life for this minute or two, a small flicker in his eye registering to me that there was at least the tiniest recognition that I was once his friend. I'm glad to see it. It makes this encounter all the sweeter. The only improvement would be if—never mind, it was happening. Four or five of my boys roll up, on their way to get more beer over at the liquor store on Sheridan Road.

"What's up, Folks?" Jimmy3 asks. "Do you know these pussies?"

"No," I say. "I don't."

"They trespassing?" he asks.

"I do believe they are," I say.

"Gotta pay a toll, then," Jimmy2 says.

"A *tax*," I say. "It's a *tax*, Jimmy."

"Sure, Midget. You're so uptight sometimes," Jimmy2 says.

"Yeah, bro," Jimmy3 says. "True."

"You wanna say 'pedantic' there, homes?" I say.

"Whatever," the Jimmys say.

"In this case, it's an *asshole tax*," I say.

They laugh a little.

"Sure," Jimmy2 says. "An *asshole* tax. Whatever you gotta do."

"So, assholes," Jimmy1 says, "you got the tax?"

One of the college boys looks at me, expectantly or pathetically, I ain't judging.

"Well, do you?" I ask.

"Yeah, sure, *Teddy*," he says.

"Good for you," I say. "Pay the man."

They hand two cases of Old Style tallboys over to the Jimmys.

"See? Was that so hard?" I ask.

Heads down, they walk out of the scrub and grass in a sad-ass college-boy processional.

My glow flares a little brighter.

Waves crash and roar, crash and roar.

The thunders hug me in a way I'll love for the rest of my days.

5. WHERE'S THE SUNSHINE?

'm trying to get out the door of this joint with some spicy chicken and these rice and beans, but then I really look at the person who just took my order and my money and I see a yellow-haired girl with "DORITOS" tattooed across her pale, thin wrist. Holy shit they like to smoke weed in this town.

The tattoo thing is weird. When I was a kid, not too many people had tattoos. All right, really, only three kinds of people—carnies, ex-cons, and gangbangers. That's it. So, if you committed to tattoos early on and you didn't grow up next to a freak show, okay, to the official freak show, then you were a crook of some kind or another. But now, everyone has tattoos. It's kind of embarrassing, really.

I look down at my own tattooed hands, the ones I thought would never live past thirty (because who the fuck would tattoo their *hands* for christ's sake? Most tattooists wouldn't touch your hands or face back in the day), and I think about my old limo-driver friend Vassily.

Vassily and me are friends. We didn't start out that way, sure, but it's okay. He's a linguist, a professor who took the Russians up on their détente-inflected offer to leave the Soviet Union and eventually settled in West Rogers Park, somewhere near (I always picture him there, anyway) the sign that read "Save Soviet Jewry" by Devon Avenue, except here in the States, instead of teaching bored rich kids how to diagram sentences in Old Norse or whatever, he drives a limo. Once he was just my driver for a night in Chicago, took me where I needed to go *and* made me laugh. These days, though, we hang out and shit, drive around in his limo together. I still like to sit in the back sometimes. He usually doesn't care when I do and uses the opportunity to smoke much weed, which is Vassily's thing, but not mine. Whatever.

This Tuesday, though, he seems super high, and I'm a little worried, even for him. We're sitting in the parking lot of a crappy hamburger place on the North Side, White Castle or Rally's or something, anyway, on one of Chicago's sensible streets, the ones that angle out like spokes from downtown. Elston, Milwaukee, Archer, Ogden, all of those streets started out as "Indian Trails," and whether they're Potawatomi or Illinois or Miami, they're the best way to get around town quick. I'm in the back seat drinking beers and he's up front, coughing from the cheap paper he rolls his joints with and brushing the floating ash off his bargain black suit coat.

"Hey, Vassily. You hungry, man?" I say, trying to cut through his buzz a little. I want to buy my friend lunch.

"This trick fucking question you are asking," he says. "I am from Soviet fucking Union, man. I stand in line one time six fucking days for a molded grape. Yes. Vassily is hungry, jackass greasy face Injun sometime best friend. But, this shit, this 'hamburger' inside roach motel here not even edible for poor Vassily ugly fuck dog back in Odessa."

Guess he's not that high, just super pensive. "Deep Thoughts with Vassily." I shudder a little.

I laugh and say, "Head up Elston. Let's go eat for real then."

"Up Elston? To where fucking Polacks live? So Vassily can die young and beautiful? Why TeddyBear so mean poor Vassily? Have only tried to be friend, but no, it is now death for Vassily. Death by jealous Polack hand. Such sad ending."

"No. It's a hillbilly place."

"Oh. Why didn't just say so?"

We drive slow, take it easy. The sights slide by, and we don't talk, just take it all in. The neighborhoods go from a little grimy to a lot of dull, postwar construction in all its utilitarian glory that rages up and down blocks full of delis with potato sausage–packed windows and bars swinging *Zimne Piwo* Old Style signs out front. We make a quick right after about fifteen minutes of travel agencies and Western Unions splashed in Polish and Spanish that eventually fade back into English and park this big black Lincoln kind of in the bus stop in front of our destination, a little big-windowed place that sits at the end of one of those weird-angled corner buildings. Vassily hangs the checkerboard hatband from a cop hat off the rearview mirror and locks the door. "Fuck it," he tells me. "My sister doesn't blow this fat married pig in squad car on last day of each month so that Vassily can pay for parking."

We look around, eyes adjusting from the greyed-out but still-bright snowbanks and the not-as-weak-as-you'd-think winter sun. The floor is that so-small white six-sided tile with the black grout, and there's fake spoiled-pudding-colored paneling under the counter where seven or eight red vinyl stools sag under the sad and solid weight of a thousand Chicago sausage-bred asses, and there's paneling on the walls above the booth where we sit, and it runs down the wall into the hall and darkens the bathrooms and the stock room but no, it's all just old brown wood-grained contact paper peeling under the haze of the shitty fluorescent lights that always give me a headache so I swallow something out of my change pocket to fight that ahead of time and I slouch into the booth and struggle out of the coat I should've taken off when I was still standing. Vassily looks at me and just shakes his head.

"For smart guy sometimes make dumb decision, Feo."

"I know, man. One of those days."

"Talk to Vassily."

"Hold on. Here comes the waitress."

"Waitress? All these fucking chicks you call 'waitress' have hand tattoo like harden Moscow criminal, man. What the fuck kind place taking Vassily to? Thought Vassily and Feodor have agreement. Vassily drive slow around corner so Teddy not spill horrible malt beverage, and Vassily not perish by fist of treacherous American redneck girl."

"Shit. They won't hurt you. You won't die today," I say.

"The 'waitress' girls?" Vassily makes dramatic quote marks in the air with his oddly scarred hands when he says "waitress." "Vassily not afraid of 'waitress' (again with the quotes) in this joint. Vassily afraid of place in back that yell around and make 'food' (he loves an air quote) for unsuspecting customer."

"Come on, Vassily. Don't be a dick. They have jelly omelets on the menu, and they deep fry most of the shit they serve. Or grill the piss right out of it. You ever have scrambled eggs and fried bologna?"

"Only when first come to this deprive capitalist funhouse and forced to, like some ill-behave dog. Why Teddy eat like strange kind wild hillbilly?"

"You better hush that pretty mouth of yours, Vassily," I say. "Big Verdell gone come out from behind the counter and fill it with something you might not like."

"Stop salty talking, Feodor writer asshole. Vassily not comfortable with easy American sex conversation. Have no boundary this country."

"Hahahaha. Fuck you, Vassily. How's that?"

"Asshole."

"Okay. Here she is. Knock it off."

It's Misty. She eyes us up. Appears to be in the mood for zero shit. I look over at Vassily, duck lip it, and roll my eyes up and over. He shakes his head a little. I worry about this guy's social capabilities.

"Uh, Vassily have eggs, but no goddamn bologna. Toast bread. Coffee."

"Sweetie," the waitress says, "I don't know who the hell Vassily is, but that ain't him across from you and you're gonna have to speak English if you want me to put in an order for you."

I look in her face, maybe for a beat too long. Wow. What a life. I say, "Sorry about that. He's a little foolish."

"Oh," she says. "Sorry about the cussing, then."

"No worries, dear," I say. "Can you give us a few more minutes? And a couple of coffees?"

"Sure thing, hon," she says. "I'll be right back."

Vassily gives me this look.

"What the fuck does 'foolish' mean?" he says. "This mean retard?"

"No, man. Don't worry about it," I say.

"Oh, Vassily worry about it. Is she some kind strange Polack? One having weird American hillbilly accent? Vassily felt very judged. Is not comfortable. Probably two minute until giant Stanislaus brother come, make Uki jelly from poor Vassily organs."

"This 'not comfortable' thing," I say (yeah, full air quotes). "You're like a delicate flower, Vassily. What the fuck has happened to you?"

"Did you see her have burn on hand like has been used for ashtray. This bullshit, I say, because beautiful flower tattoo now burnt. Did Teddy not see this? Mr. Writer, Mr. Observant?"

"I told you I'm not a writer, man. You're just trying to make some shitty Russian connections with your man Dostoevsky because my first name is Theodore, not Feodor. And you know I'm a Gogol fan anyway, so knock it off."

"This Gogol thing, weak, Feo. This *Overcoat* love you have, not good. Short story for weakling. Men write novel, not tiny cute story."

For the second time in about five minutes I say, "Fuck you, Vassily."

Vassily must've scared her off, or it's time for a shift change, because all of a sudden we're gonna get a new waitress. I see her from behind at first, looking at Misty pointing over at us and shaking her head. The new girl, I wonder if it's that one waitress I had last time I was here. That waitress had had an accident, one that left her with an eyepatch. On which she had painted a butterfly, a mourning cloak to remind her of the eyelash thing she used to do with her daughter at bedtime. She had been putting on makeup doing that weird thing girls do when they put on makeup, wiping at her eye while pulling down at the lower lid.

And that's when the other car hit.

I know this because I asked her.

Unlike Vassily, I really have no filter.

But it's not her. It's someone newer, someone else. She heads over to our booth.

She's beautiful. Truly beautiful, the woman I always fall for, the one just less than the perfect that can only be made by the Creator, like the single black ten-cut in the beadwork, the one with the fucked-up teeth, not all crooked, but like the canine is trying to mug the lateral incisor, and that number ten tooth just ain't having it, and when she smiles just right, you can see their enameled struggle going down in a way that makes her absolutely perfect to you. She is that last flower, the one running on Indian time, the bright-pink whorl on the brown-grey rosebush, the one with the coppery leaves and the barky shadow-sketched outline, its last lone bud making it all the more achingly beautiful. The most beautiful. And now she's here.

I can't talk.

Goddamnit.

But my eyes can move.

I look over at Vassily.

He jumps in:

"Wait. Do you know this man?"

She looks at him. Looks at me. I shrink a little further into the booth.

"Obviously you do not know this great man," Vassily continues. "He is literary giant, is great writer, is famous. How you not know Feodor?"

She says, "What'll you have? You changing your order, or are you still good with eggs and the 'toast bread' (she gives him the air quotes)?"

"No. No. This man deserve introduction. Please, miss. Miss. Hear poor Vassily humble words."

Humble words. This motherfucker, Vassily. I'm embarrassed.

Vassily, though, he's tryna. For me. What a guy.

Except she's not buying it. Yup. Of course, now I'm even deeper in love.

"Vassily. Let's go."

"What, man? Are talking such bullshit, now."

"Dude. It's okay. Let's go," I say.

"But Vassily working Ukrainian love magic. Teddy will be having the sex any minute now, while poor Vassily sadly but happily eating toast bread and waiting to warm up car, while greasy-face friend making humpty hump in back room."

She gives him the death stare, but he keeps smiling like no one is there but me and him.

"Nah. I'm good," I say.

"What the fuck talking about, man?" he says.

"It's cool."

"No. Is not cool. Fuck you, man. This brooding bullshit too much sometime."

She's clearly uncomfortable. I want to tell her it's okay, and please don't freak out, and when do you get off work, and have you ever been to Italy or the Badlands or even fucking Muncie, anywhere but here because I want to take you there and never come back, but I don't do any of that since I'm incapacitated.

Vassily goes on. "Well fuck this then," he says. "Let's go to car."

I put a ten on the table, cause, shit, I don't know what else to do.

"Let's go, idiot," he says.

She looks into my face, judges my past, calculates my future, maybe sees something I missed. She walks away. I watch her do it.

"Hey, idiot. Want get high?"

Jesusfuckinchrist. I can't believe this.

"No," I say. Shit. "Sit. Shut up."

"Oh no. Not telling Vassily shut up sit down. You be fucking quiet right now, mister. Put money back in pocket. Vassily stepping outside to hit this joint, then coming back to decide rest of beautiful day plan. This stand up sit down shut up giving Vassily headache. Is like Catholic Church or something."

He heads through the door and I turn away, look for her immediately. She leans on the gold-flecked white Formica counter, reads over her order tickets. Of course that piece of hair falls from behind her ear and over her eye when she does it, that piece you'll always remember when you describe how you fell in love with your grand-kids' *unci* the day they met, the story they'll never get tired of hear-ing as long as you make that moony face and laugh like you do when you tell it.

"What on paper, Mr. Not Writing?" Vassily returns, smells like a skunk pissed on his red, white, and blue shoes. Just so you know, Vassily has worn bowling shoes since moving to America. "Is nothing this comfortable ever made Russia," he tells me. "Or beau-tiful," he likes to add.

"Nothing. Just a note."

"Shut it. Stop this bullshitting of Vassily. Give to me."

He reads it. Out loud. The prick.

In that accent of his. Hahaha. He reads:

We make our way to the front, now bearing these gifts at the head of the room. When we share, we do our best to give everything we have, but in those moments when all of it is rejected, when the world says this is not enough, our eyes widen, not from pain, but from searching for that littlest bit of light that's just been lost. Some-times, in that deepening of the eyes, the sharing of the soul, the love comes back to us, and then, too, our eyes widen, but the better to receive that gift, that return of heart, that reason, that hum, that scratch on the paper in the night in the dark, in the weakest of light, the why we do what we do.

He looks at me. Eyes a little wider. And says,

"You motherfucker. Now making Vassily want punch Feodor face. And self in balls. You are jagoff."

I laugh.

We eat.

Vassily eats the grape-jelly omelet I talked him into. "What the fuck! This delicious!" he says, high as a fucking kite, choking on "toast bread" and asking for more tea.

I pick at my fried bologna. The thing about it is you have to eat it quick, right when you get it, or it turns weird, things congeal, desire . . . slips. I smoke cigarettes instead, drink coffee. Pretend I'm looking out the window when all I can do is slip glances of her sideways in the smudgy glass, her face lightly overlaying the underlying snowbanks, crusted in black on their uneven tops, tiny copies of the Alps, salted rivers and ash defining their peaks. Vassily talks under his breath, compliments the food, misses his mom, speaks Ukrainian words whose meaning I'll never know— translations will always be insufficient when we work to describe love. If I had a mom to miss, I would, right along with Vassily, but instead I wish it was July, cause for some of us the only warm hug you get is from a slow summer rain.

We finish eating. Well, Vassily finishes eating, and I drink coffee, steal away looks at my future wife, kill a pack of Newports. It sleets a little, and then the sun comes out and tilts quicker than I thought it would, the darkened light of a late North Side winter pushing against the buzzing fluorescents here in the restaurant. I throw the ten back on the table. The best light in the world waits outside. It's where we head.

"Sit in front seat with poor Vassily."

"No."

"Goddamit, Feo. Am not your fucking driver today, man."

Shit.

"Alright, man. Calm down," I say.

I hop up front with Vassily. It's a fuckin' pigsty. There's chip bags and shit, pop cans and candy wrappers, and everything is covered in ash, like maybe Vassily is the Uki word for volcano.

"What the hell happens up here, Vassily?" I ask. "Jesus Christ, man. This place is a fucking dump. You need to clean this shit up."

"Think of this as proof Vassily success. This trash Vassily pay to have picked up by other less fortunate lumpenproletariat, contribute to American dream for other miserable fuck somewhere, have car detailed Bensonville, Franklin Park. Hell, maybe Berwyn."

I turn to my left, look at his not-smiling face, reply with my own slitted stare.

"Hahahaha! Vassily joke! Fuck Berwyn. Just kid!"

I laugh too. "Ya motherfucker. Just drive."

Vassily heads east toward the lake, takes Foster all the way down. It's dumpy, dumpier, dumpiest. By the time we get over by Edgewater Hospital, the boarded-up site of my birth, it's just fucked.

"You're bumming me out, man," I say. "Hang a left up here and take Clark Street up toward Rogers. We can go to Leone or Jarvis Beach or something."

"Teddy needs to stop drinking so much daytime," he says, leaning into the turn. "Am not going to fucking beach in winter. Vassily might be from Soviet Union, and once try to fuck polar bear, but is not swimming Lake fucking Michigan wintertime. This crazy talk."

I crack the window and light a smoke from a fresh pack.

"No. We're good. No swimming, man. Just looking," I say.

"Who is bumming out who now," Vassily says, "with a visit to cold lonely beach for 'looking' (air quotes)? Looking what? Sadness? Is already much sad here in front seat right now. Does Teddy need ride back to diner; back to booth so can moony face over new waitress? How come did not talk more? Get phone number? Use writer-man charm? Vassily much worried now. Does not like friend maudlin bullshit."

"Fuck, man. Just drive. Let's cruise."

"Smoke a joint?"

"No thanks. Pass," I say.

"Suit self," says Vassily, and he pulls one out from the elastic band on the driver side visor, the one that's supposed to hold your parking receipt, or a valet ticket, or some kind of memento from a life someone else will get to live. It looks like he rolled this joint in the cheap newsprint from the free weekly. I watch him dig for a light for a minute ("Having matches somewhere," he says, patting his side pockets and digging deep into his black polyester blazer), and when none appear, I pull out a lime green Cricket and hold it lit to his face. He jumps a little, and then he pulls the flame to the joint. Acrid paper smoke fills the car and then heads toward the window I have vented over on my side, giving me a chance to huff up all that nasty smell on its way out the crack just above my head. Vassily coughs like he's got the consumption, takes another quick hit, holds it in, and then rolls his eyes over my way while he keeps his head straight in the seat, never moving it a hair. He's glazed and blazed out, has that grin going on.

"Pay attention to the road, man. Stop looking at me," I say. "You're freaking me out."

"Worry too much, Feo. Have got this. Vassily is professional driver, man. Relax."

I do. We move north pretty fast; there aren't too many cars at all. No one really wants to be stuck in this neighborhood as the sun heads down, and I think I saw the bus driver change his sign to read "Out of Service" just because. But Clark is a big, wide street, and up here, when it's deserted this way, the sun setting out in the suburbs somewhere, the light hitting the top floors of the yellow-bricked buildings and slashing off the glass windows while the purpled darkness pools in the wide canyon floor below, it's just beautiful.

We pass Devon, and Pratt, Morse, and Touhy. I point over to the left. "Vassily. Check it out." I show him some graffiti on a wall that I did. It was supposed to say:

with Kings written upside down (as a mark of disrespect), but I was so drunk and so used to writing it upside down that I accidentally did the Kings a solid when I hung off the roof and tagged the building across from Zayre's in fine fashion where it stood for so long they eventually took over the neighborhood and it fit right in:

with the cross and the bunny painted over at some point. Shit.

Vassily laughs at me. Eats the roach left from the joint he's been smoking on again off again. I lean my arm out and lob the quart bottle of Old Style backwash I've been nursing over the top of the car at the offending building and then we're quick at Jarvis so I yell, "Take a right!" and we gun it toward the lake.

I can smell the water before I can see it, the dying sky out over the lake like unpolished steel, still sooty and flat, but with sharp edges that pick up the last bits of light in the day. Vassily is so high I'm not sure if he's awake, so I poke him with my finger, the one with the cross tattooed on it, and say,

"Hey—got any of that coke left from last night?"

"Sure," he says. "Feo and Vassily do nice fat line."

And we do.

Four or five more times. Vassily grabs an old plastic cup out of the holder in the door and finds the fixin's for Greyhounds down in this magic console between us in the front seat. I finish off a couple warmish Mickey's Big Mouths I find in that console. We listen to the water, watch the light leave the day for night. After a while I tell Vassily let's go, let's head south, pick up Lake Shore Drive and go down to Michigan Avenue and look at the lights or something.

We head out in the now-shadowed night, kinda fucked up, kinda listening to the radio, kinda singing too loud to whatever classic rock they're playing on the Loop, the limo and its fine sound system wasted on this shit. We make the turn at Hollywood and hit the Drive. We cruise and both try to see the last light off the endless glassy lake, see what's out there that's better than whatever's here. I think we drift a bit. Then me and Vassily, we hit the embankment and roll that limo, the big Linc turning in the cold iced air, windows shattering and safety glass tinkling down, and we come to rest on our side looking out at the lake, our breath steaming out into the night's winter dark, one wide beam pouring down from the moon onto the water, the glow it throws back laying bare our petty sins for all to see, transgressions long and shady, but the evening rush screams past, caring even less than we do. We just laugh, alive in the moment, so sure that sun's coming up tomorrow.

6. TECUMSEH AT THE TOWER

As to boundaries, the Great Spirit above knows no boundaries, nor will his red children acknowledge any.

—TECUMSEH

What is this?

"It's a memorial to the Battle of Ft. Dearborn. They used to call it the Ft. Dearborn Massacre, but it, uh, got changed."

Hmmm.

"Mmmhmmm."

Tell me more about it.

"Sure thing. Let's walk, Grandfather."

We head north up Michigan Avenue toward Water Tower Place, the wind warm and surprisingly from the east, bringing the smells of the lake our way. Bad day for alewives.

I show him a picture on my phone of the original monument.

Hmmm. He doesn't look Potawatomi to me.

I like that he doesn't mention the phone thing. Cool.

I say,

"The artist used Short Bear, a Sicangu, who was being held up at Ft. Sheridan after the murders at Čaŋkpé Opí Wakpa, at Wounded Knee, as a model for Black Partridge in the sculpture."

His eyes go liquid for a bit.

The pain in both faces . . .

The whole place sure looks different than when I was a kid, and I can't imagine what it looks like to him now. Shit, the river doesn't even flow in the same direction. We head over the bridge and half-way across, then he stops me, looks at the sign.

They named this bridge for Point de Sable? They spelled his name wrong.

"They did." I had forgotten he could read English.

He was a good man, fair at least. He married a Potawatomi woman, didn't he? An ancestor of the Pokagon we heard about for a while.

"That's true, Grandfather," I say.

I'm surprised the Americans would allow a monument to a black man.

"Times have changed. A little, anyway."

Hmmm. He raises an eyebrow.

"Yeah. Not much," I agree.

But there are many Indian people here now, in this city.

"You're right. They had a program starting seventy-five years or so ago, called 'Relocation.' They tricked a lot of Native folks into moving to the city. Places like Chicago and Denver, Minneapolis and Los Angeles. They said it was for jobs and opportunities. I think it was because they were afraid of communism. America survives best when they have something to be afraid of. And the vaguer, the better."

They are a fearful people, Grandson.

"And cruel, Grandfather. That's something we never forget. Still see."

There are Indians, but where are the Potawatomi? This was their territory.

"Well there's a park named for them, Grandfather."

And that's all?

I tell him to the best of my memory:

According to Chief Simon Pokagon's 1899 article, "The Fort Dearborn battle has been denounced by the dominant race as a brutal massacre, regardless of its many individual acts of mercy and kindness. In this wholesale slaughter, not one white man stretched out a hand to save a single soul." I've paraphrased it a little.

He replies,

Pokagon was an observant man. And wise to have learned English. It was the only language they would respect you in, then.

The brass buttons on his Redcoat officer's jacket flash bright in the early summer sun, narrow my pupils.

"You're right. I've made it a point to be well-versed in it myself."

That's good, Grandson. Creator has shown you a worthwhile path.

"I think so. I do my best."

It's all any of us can do, what we are supposed to do.

He spots a street sign, continues, eyebrows raised:

I see they named a street after that traitor to our English allies. I should have done more to help our confederates hang him when he changed his allegiance to the Americans. Kinzie expended quite a bit of effort trying to arm our brothers to fight for them, afterward. If I recall, a granddaughter of his tried to rewrite the history of this place, make their family out to be heroes. It would appear it worked for a bit, at least.

"It's unfortunate," I say. "But it's everywhere in this country the invaders now control. They have a singular way of recasting history to make themselves righteous victors in what they portray as their creator's war on all of us." I surprise myself with all this formal English coming out of my mouth.

Grandson, we saw that writ large on their faces in every meeting, every council, every treaty attempt they ever proposed. Versions of it appeared on the faces of their British relatives, no matter how hard they tried to deny it. These whites are eternally famished for land and divine approval of their thievery. Anishinaabe deemed it Wendigo, and Sioux called it Wasicu, but in the end it was all the same—a never-sated thirst for *more*, and nothing else, no matter what the more might be. So very sad, but so very destructive for our people.

I think this is some heavy shit to be laying on a kid, but I say,

"We're doing what we can to fight it, though the burden is heavy." What the fuck is that? I'm talking like it's the 1820s or something.

What do you think your ancestors carried, to ensure you'd be here today?

He's right, of course. We drive around in cars to ceremony, fill buckets of water with ease at the side of houses for our sweats, turn up the heat or the air conditioner, buy ground buffalo at the grocery store. Cry around online about mascots and ignore regular assaults on our sovereignty, we who fight over blood quantum and dogshit percaps and ignore traditional kinship and ways of knowing on the regular. We're shit descendants and worse ancestors most of the time. I have no reply.

Which works out, cause he's super tradish, doesn't remark on my silence, let's me have it. We walk along. I watch him watch people. After a while he says,

Do people really have so much that they throw out food, yet feel so little they ignore their starving relatives?

"Every day, Grandfather. Every day."

It was hard in our time, to be sure, but I prefer those days to these ones of excess and foolishness.

"I do, too. Or at least I think I would."

I'm not sure you would make it, Grandson.

"I'd try, anyway."

That I'm sure of. He smiles, pats me on the shoulder.

"I appreciate that," I say, marveling at his reach through the years.

We've been standing on the bridge, talking in front of the Du Sable plaque. I look around at all the people rushing back and forth, franchise coffee cups gripped in stressed-out hands, beautiful weather ignored, hundreds of eyes never meeting each other. He stares out over the river, his gaze set beyond the lake, covering hundreds of miles and thousands of years. I watch him watching, amazed at all he has seen, has known, will know.

"Grandfather, can I ask you something."

His hands rub at the stone balustrade, taking and imparting warmth at the same time.

What is it?

"Do we find out why, what, when we make the journey?"

Do you believe we do?

"I do. It's what we do, right? What else is there to believe? The ancestors' road is our way."

There's so much more than that. You have to dream bigger.

"Bigger than the universe?"

The universe? You shouldn't think so small, Grandson.

I wish I could even begin to imagine.

I put my own hands on the stone, stare deep into the horizon.

He watches me do it, smiles, and puts his hand on my shoulder.

I look deeper into the world, my vision stretching into a twisted past, unwinding to a future we both could see, only one of us understanding.

For now.

7. THE LAMB

> Greater love has no one than this:
> to lay down one's life for one's friends.
>
> —JOHN 15:13

We smoke too much weed sometimes. Okay, lots of times, but sometimes it's just too much. We're sitting around Jimmy₁'s crib one day, trying to sneak pieces of the chicken his parents boil up for their spoiled dog Sheba, and listening to tunes. Jimmy₁ is an asshole about the music picks, and you better like what he likes or you're stuck. I can't stand the Who, but I respect the violin in "Teenage Wasteland" cause Jimmy₁'s old man Louie likes it. He's from Sicily so I chalk it up to the tarantella or some shit, and instead of smacking the needle across the turntable I just say,

"Turn it down."

"Fuck you," Jimmy₁ says.

Apparently, no one else likes the Who, so they shout him down. He cuts it off.

"Fuck you then," he says, puts the album back in its sleeve.

I say,

"I wanna tell you guys a story."

"Sheeeeit," they say, high as fuck. "One a them funny ones or a scary one?"

"This one is both, I think," I say. "It's a goooood one," I draw it out, high my damn self.

"Alright, Midget," JD says,

"tell us a story then motherfucker."

"Alright then," I say.

I say,

JD maws his sandwich and scans the living room for anything worth taking. The TV is a console. The VCR is a friggin' Betamax and not yet a collector's item. He throws the butt end of the bologna and cheese at the front window (he hates crusts and has trouble finishing anything of any substance, really; his lack of fortitude in that area annoys the shit out of me, but still we do stuff together) and lights a smoke.

"Teddy. What the fuck are we gonna do now?"

I stand in the living room, near the room-wide covered radiator laden with plant cuttings sitting in margarine dishes, look out the front window through the fresh mustard on the glass and out onto a grey snow-stained Damen Avenue on the North Side of Chicago. I rack focus back to the bars of light leaking through the partly open blinds. Dust mites slow roll in the sunlight like airborne sea monkeys. You could spend a lot of time watching them if you couldn't afford the watery ones from the backs of comics.

"Maybe if you had finished that goddamn sandwich you would've seen the moldy crust at the end," I say. "These people ain't got shit to steal. Fuck, man. They don't even have good bread."

This jagoff. I forgot he ate a sandwich every time he did a burglary. Ya poor-ass bastard. Some of these white boys are hardcore.

"We better get moving, I guess," he says.

"Son of a bitch. Fine. Go check the bedroom. I'll hit the medicine cabinet."

"You better share," he says.

I laugh and flick my ashes on the rug. "You know better than that. Man, I didn't even want to do this job. Think of it as your tax for making me come with."

We're cutting school. Well, actually, I'm cutting school. JD had finished eighth grade and figured that was plenty. Daytime is of course the best time to rob people who aren't home, cause they might be at work, and they might actually have some shit worth taking. Those slobs whose front doors leaked out the Price Is Right theme song didn't have much but time and the slow grind of death by boredom and napping to crappy TV, and even less to steal. They got passed by, unless you were looking for something else entirely different to while away your day, the kind of thing that sometimes made the evening news.

"I gotta take a shit, man. Let me in there, first," JD crabs at me.

I blow a smoke ring and put my cigarette out on the arm of the couch. I watch two fleas, still fucking, jump out of the way and onto my hand. I pinch them up with my thumb and a finger, nice and light, and toss them at JD. One disappears, but the other is crawling on his scabby neck. I hope it's the pregnant one, and say,

"Make it quick, jagoff. And don't touch the medicine cabinet."

"Whateeeever," he laughs, says it like he's Native. I gotta stop hanging out with him. He's picking up too much.

JD vanishes into the bathroom, still laughing. Pretty soon, though, the laughing stops and I can hear that he's actually taking a shit.

Good.

I want at that medicine cabinet.

When he does burglaries, JD makes sandwiches, takes shits, gets caught. He's not dumb, he's just . . . unsmart. And a fucking lollygagger. I'm thinking, hmmm, maybe this could work. It's late in the day, and I got kind of a bad feeling about this one, like someone could show up at any minute, but If I can get the shit I want, and get out, and he's still in here and something goes down, well that's his rep—always dicking around. Not my fault. I don't want him to get caught so much, but I want me to get caught even less.

We all make sacrifices.

I figure JD could part with a bit of his freedom if need be, better him than me and all that. JD had already parted with his dignity pretty early on, probably about the same time his pedostache started coming in, the one he probably still has, the one that just appeared like out of whole cloth or something, like a shroud of dirt. We all thought he drew it on, or glued it on. Weird.

But it wasn't the 'stache that robbed him of his dignity. Nah. It was the church.

St. Margaret Mary's. So Catholic it got two names. And an Irish monsignor. From Ireland. The real deal. Except his name was Father Thomas. That didn't sound too Irish to me. Maybe because in my head, Irish was Porky the Pig as a cop in the cartoons and was named O'Hara, like on Batman. But he had the accent and all and anyway, yeah. The church. As a descendant of converted Indians, our family had some strict ideas about who should be running things at church.

One Sunday we're in church, me and my brother. We put money in the collection plate, maybe seventy-five cents. I tried to keep it, but my brother wouldn't let me. It was the same shit when I would go to light a smoke. He was like seven, and I was nine or so. We would walk up Seeley Ave. to get to the church, and on the way there was a picture of a white-white Jesus in the window of this old lady's apartment. It was the white Jesus with the eyes, the ones that look like a deer's but really are more like a judgy assistant principal's. They say, "Oh, I see you. I know what you're doing," and other shit like that. They work on your little brother, who is terrified of the Jesus with his judgy fingers that point up in the air but are really pointing at you and his low-key glowy halo. But me? Not so much. I am, however, terrified of my father, and my brother's willingness to tell on me. The goodie-goodie little shit. We went to run away once, and as I was walking out the door, blanket, food, spot picked out, he went in to tell my ma goodbye. Jesus.

So now we're in the pew, everyone is back from the creepy transmogrification moment, and my judgy little shit brother is watching me choke back the communion wafer that to me is the same thing those flying saucer candies are made out of, the ones with the tiny colored sugar balls in the middle, or those shitty ice-cream cones you get because your ma won't buy the sugar ones, put both quarters, the two dimes, and a nickel in the collection plate, making them loud, making them count (while cussing out my cheapskate dad who couldn't even give us a dollar to put in because well he wasn't there to make the donation so fuck 'em and my boys can take the heat for me), when we see this kid struggling, fidgeting, head whipping around, all sweaty like. Holy crap. It's Baby JD. What the fuck is he doing in here?

He doesn't seem to know either, but in any instance his presence is definitely not agreeing with him. Baby JD ain't too good looking anyway, but right now he looks terrible. His mom is kinda cussing at him, hits him upside the head a couple of times. Baby JD looks down at the kneeler and shakes his head, sweat dripping out of his greasy black hair.

His shoulders heave up a little, and then a lot, like he's trying to push that little man-suit coat right off his back. He looks over at his ma and starts to get out of the pew. She takes a big swing at the side of his head, but he's too quick for her. He stumbles into the aisle like going back for seconds will save his immortal soul. Not sure why he'd want to do that, though, because if he ended up dying and going to hell, I'm pretty sure he'd finally meet his dad, who I'm definitely sure is in charge down there. He'd probably even give JD a job right off the bat.

But then Baby JD takes off down the aisle, heading for the big wooden front doors. It's one of those moments that takes on its own sense of time, slo-mos down to heartbeat speed. Light streams through the stained-glass windows and down onto the red carpet, the light pouring through the lurid stigmata even redder on the floor, yellow and blue jewels of Roman helmets and rugged crosses diffuse on the faces of the parishioners and young JD, Baby JD, jams his hand over his mouth so hard I think he might've broken his own nose, and then in the most ungodly beautiful moment JD's face erupts, shifts in violent fashion, lunges forward as three perfect sprays of sweet white puke one each for the Father, the Son, and the Holy Ghost shoot out from between his fingers and arc down onto six rows of stunned worshippers and he doesn't miss a beat, laugh-cries his way right on out those doors and into the street.

Hahaha. Fuckin' JD.

And now we do jobs together. Hilarious.

I knock on the door; make sure he's not rubbing one out in there (another trademark of his lollygagging ass).

"C'mon, JD. Let's fucking go!"

"Fuck you, Teddy. *You* check the bedroom!"

Goddamnit. I knew it. He's had a hard-on ever since he stole that .357 earlier today. I still don't know where he got it.

"I hope you break it off, you little shit!" I yell, and head over to the bedroom.

It's a terrible place, really. Bedroom-set furniture. Heavy cheap baroque buccaneer looking shit. Funky smells eep out from under the brown, orange, and cream bedspread. Cheap jewelry sits in cheaper bowls on the mirror-topped dresser. The curtains are drawn back, but the shades are down and it's way too warm. Fuck.

Dove-grey light surges around the window frames when a cloud moves out of the sun's way outside and I don't have to turn on the light as the room comes a bit brighter. I look around for pill bottles, liquor. Nothing. Toss a couple of drawers in search of weed, quick-stashed cash. Getting shut out here, I yell, "JD, hurry the fuck up!"

I check the closet. Shoes that haven't been worn in ten years litter the floor, still hanging on mostly as pairs, but like couples who are kinda tired of each other, people you see where Jimmy's ma's a waitress. They're at the bar together, but they sit apart a little and talk to other people. Clothes made out of fabrics that are probably illegal now crowd the saggy bar that stretches from wall to wall, dust on the shoulders of shirts that'll be in style twenty years from now. I pull the string for the overhead light, see it's an old bathtub ball chain hanging from a bare bulb fixture. I follow it up to a socket on a braided cord that drops down from a ceiling that's higher than I expected.

I look back above the door and see a spot not covered in cobwebs. There's something taped to the angled ceiling.

I grab hold of it and take it down. I pull all this tape off. It's a little .32 magnum, the one where the grips are the biggest part of the gun. It's not dusty or anything, but I blow on it anyway, can smell the propellant. I stuff it in the waistband of my baggies, under this Bad Company T-shirt, the one with the rainbow glitter weed leaf in the middle. I could sell this piece. Or use it. Nice grab.

The rest of the closet is a fucking bust. Photo books that might get pulled out some drunken night, the old man trying to get his tired wife in the sack—"Remember when I looked like this?!"— and hoping she won't remember what he looks like now, how his belly sags like her interest in hearing him bitch about work, but maybe they could fuck this one time at the kitchen table, and eat leftover pizza after, and pass out naked, on *top* of the sheets, dreaming of better days, or the way things used to be, like when they first met.

I find his tame-ass porno mags, or maybe they're hers. Or both. People are into all kinds of shit nowadays. Whatever. There's a few more photo albums. I decide these folks need a vacation. Jesus Christ. Looks like the only place they ever go is to her ma's house, which, near as I can tell, is on a part of the South Side that never gets any sun, like Bridgeport. I'm kinda glad I'm taking the gun because I'm pretty sure it's just a matter of time before this guy shoots himself.

I'm tempted to light the clothes and whole house on fire, do these people a solid, burn out their shitty memories and make them get some new ones, make them make some new ones, remember life is short and that's why it's so precious, but I'm not feeling particularly generous, or helpful, and besides, their taste in furniture sucks, and I'm pretty sure they'd just replace it with the same crap. I mean for real; the guy has short-sleeved dress shirts and sans-a-belt pants. C'mon.

I'm getting a little sweaty here in this tiny shitbox, and I back out of the closet and shut the door, a quick flash of the sad couple behind my eyes along with all the bright future denied to them because I didn't feel like burning down their accumulated failures. Man, I'm a lazy prick.

Well that's about it for this room. One last place to check.

Under the bed. I yank up the edge of the sheet and

there's a chick's face inches from mine. Big brown eyes bug out, the whites shot through with burst capillaries. Mouth shut tight. Looking right back at me.

Fuck.

I jump back and feel my head clock on something hard, metal.

It's that .357 in JD's hand.

"Something under there, Teddy?" he throws out through clenched teeth.

Motherfucker.

"You need to calm down, JD," I say.

"I don't need to do jack shit, Teddy."

He's right about that. But I say anyway, "Man, just tell me what happened. Maybe we can figure this out."

"Nah. Fuck that. He wasn't supposed to be home. I came by this morning, when everyone should've been out of the house, off to work and school and shit. But here he was."

"So what happened, man?" *(He? I think.)*

"I ain't telling you shit, man," JD says.

I needed to know, cause when I came through here a few hours ago, there wasn't anybody home, at least no one that I knew of. I had broken in through the old coal door off the pantry on the back porch and immediately went through the medicine cabinet in the rear bathroom. Snagged two bottles of syrup and a junky old pill bottle with six Quaaludes in it. There was probably more here, but since I got a little excited and chugged a bottle of that syrup on the spot and popped one of the 'ludes, and I had already taken two Darvocets earlier (start the day right with a healthy breakfast and all that shit) I couldn't really remember when I woke up down in the basement of this old building if I finished tossing the place. Or what I did after that syrup kicked in. Which is why I was back here, JD in tow. Fuck. Was she already under the bed then? Sonofabitch.

"JD. Who is that, man?"

"Who?"

"The chick under the bed."

"What chick under the bed?"

"There's a chick under the bed, man."

"Fuck you."

"There is. I'm telling you, JD."

"There might be a *dude* under the bed, but there ain't no chick, that's for sure."

"See for yourself," I say.

I slow back out of the way, crouching low and keeping my hands out at my sides. JD kind of points the gun my way, bends down to look under the bed

and her hands shoot out, grab up handfuls of that greasy black hair, and drag his face to hers. He squeezes off a shot that explodes a dresser drawer and digs deep somewhere in the wall behind it just as he drops the gun. I'm knocked off balance by both the loudness of the magnum in this small, close room, and the holy-fuck strength of the girl under the bed, the one who's looking up at me now, the last bit of JD's nose stuck just inside her wet wet mouth, the one with the clacking teeth and the quick licking tongue.

What the fuck.

JD's not making any sounds at all, and I can smell piss, then shit. I see the pistol way too close to her, and right at the ah fuck moment, I remember the .32 in my jock. I grab at the automatic and think I gotta get the hell outta here. The chick's not really moving, just click-clacking them teeth, chewing up that last bit of JD's face, and staring at me. She's kind of pretty, and I have a thing for crooked teeth, but I slide the gun up real slow and put a lucky shot right in the middle of her forehead. The bone folds in on itself, leaks some of its contents out the back into the folds of the dusty comforter, and her brown eyes dim, the whites filling a deep red. She rests there on the floor, partway out from under the bed, what's left of her face just visible behind the ruins of JD's, one of her hands stretched out, a bloody hank of JD's hair still attached to a chunk of his scalp entwined in her slim white fingers. Dead as a fucking doornail for the last time.

The clacking sound keeps going, but her teeth ain't moving. I creep up close and look real hard, just to make sure, my face inches from hers, the gun up close by our heads. Nope. No movement at all. Her last breath of course smells like death, but yeah. Nothing.

I look over at her hand (gross as fuck) and I can see JD's hair sort of moving. I look up toward the back of the room, and there's a fan going, the intake pulling at the plastic end of the cord for the blinds, and I think that's the clacking, but it doesn't sound right, doesn't line up quite the way it should, and then the clacking is right up close behind me and that's where her brother went, the one JD thought he killed and stuffed under the bed, the brother of the sister who went looking for him, went to help him when she heard the little burglar shoot him earlier, shoot him and try to hide him.

I smell death again, way too close, and then I remember the gun in my hand, the one now under my chin. I wait a split second for the clacking to come closer.

We all make sacrifices.

"You motherfucker!"

"Daaaaaayumn!"

"Hahahaha! Good story!"

"Wait. That was about this crib, wasn't it?!" Jimmyı is all fired up.

JD says, "Is there really a gun in that closet? I'ma check right now!"

"I wouldn't go in there if I was you,"

I say.

8. BY THE SLICE

They seemed to be in love, but maybe it was the pecan pie. Even under the buzz of fluorescent lights, pie makes life so much more bearable, enhances everyone's natural beauty. Or maybe one of them was paying the other to be there. Either way, they were a couple for now.

She didn't talk so much as she moved her mouth around her words like a sleep-clinic escapee. That her brown eyes whirred around as if the batteries that might have operated them were starting to crap out only added to the sense that some technician needed to fine-tune her face, at least adjust the tracking. Her wide-strapped dress looked homemade, the cream and burgundy floral pattern better at home in a set of drapes than in the wrinkly pile of heavy fabric that crawled across her thin shoulders, crushed her dirty-blonde hair, accented her skin that looked more like smoked bluefish than a wrap to contain a human and its attendant soul.

He had no trouble talking, or at least making the effort, definitely had tried too hard once anyway, spoke to the wrong people maybe, by the looks of him. His clothes lumpy and shapeless from the chest down, the grunge of a grey hooded flannel all olive-striped and red-orange piled around his neck, brown hair greasy and splayed on the grubby fabric belying the clean crisp earnest of his speech, his green-blue eyes turning inward and down toward a mouth he seemed to hardly believe could contain so many words and a tongue so restless. And someone had cut that impulsive tongue of his just so, not in a way that affected his speech but still in a way that you could see the two split ends fighting to work independently behind his yellowy teeth, and his words came out fucked up not because they were impeded in any way but because you were spending too much effort on looking at his moray eel mouth and not enough on listening to what his scruffed and ashy slack face was struggling to say.

The two of them grummumbled into their fat slices of pie, pecan and pumpkin, the too much sugar of them turning to small points of diamonded glass and glowing crystals under the hot amber lights, and they picked and scratched at each other, just like everyone else in this tired but busy diner, one located not on some grimy street or out there off an endless interstate but in an urban strip mall, set down in the middle of a city whose main export was probably rain, the chalky stains of ten thousand storms streaking the windows that looked out into misted alleys and the too-close faces of hungry drunks who maybe just wanted a bite or two. The talking wasn't the thing the quiet couple were into, though, and the air around them changed when their hands and fingers touched here and there as they reached for their cold coffee or thin paper napkins, or really, each other, their rustles and murmurs flowing up and into a just-visible stream that moved warm air and muffled words and open lust and so-sharp smells above the crowded bloodred vinyl booths and past the plastic plants that worked like fading green dust filters and heavy-leafed cobweb holders.

"What is your fucking problem?" he mumbled at her.

"I am g ng s k. I d 't fe l g d," she mouthed back.

"You're always fucking sick," his tongues twisted away.

"F k y u, as o l ," her mouth squished, as she reached to pick at the dirty beds of his nails.

He smiled and massaged her raw, red knuckles with his thumb and first two fingers, his last two raised in a canted peace sign.

She coughed and spit up a little, slurred a shy "I l v y u," and covered the bottom of her face with one hand as she then hacked away for a full half minute or so.

He never flinched, just kept rubbing her other hand.

"You okay?" he asked when her rail-slat chest finally stopped heaving.

"Y p," she winked, and chugged her whole cup of cooled coffee.

"Man," he sighed, and smiling, softly shook his head, blinking at his luck and his love.

She grinned wide, and he could see that favorite flaw of his in her face, her left lateral incisor trying to strong arm its canine neighbor, those dental imperfections gifted by Creator forever his downfall. Amazing, he thought, almost out loud.

Some folks communicate in small quiet gestures, others, nah. My ma and dad? Well, for Dad that was usually a no. Gesture-wise, there was lots of loud, pinched-lip, set-jaw nose breathing. Usually with my old man, though, there was no talking at all. But sometimes there were words, like these. Him: "Close your mouth, shit for brains"—to my six-year old brother; "Close your mouth when you chew, whatthefuckiswrongwithyou"—this, to my oldest but still four-year-old sister on the occasional Sunday when he'd bother to eat with us; "Close your fucking mouth!"—this, just this.

Hahaha. He had a real problem with that mouth breathing thing. "Jeeezus Caahrist," he liked to say.

My ma, though, lots of gestures, cause she smoked eight thousand cigarettes a day and drank ten thousand cups of coffee. She vibrated through my field of vision, and when she raised a hand it was like when the picture starts to go out on an old TV, like a black-and-white Zenith, and when it cracks and whips, the old man makes you wiggle the antenna until it stops, and then you just stand there holding it.

With your fucking mouth shut.

But neither my ma or dad were really communicating. That's not what their words were doing. At least not with each other. Us kids? We knew what was happening. These two idiots were building a prison around us, the walls they put up between themselves fenced *us* in, closed our horizons and gave us nowhere to go. They made it colder in the winter and hotter in the summer, climate-dictated misery we tried to be kids in, while we wound up proxy-waging bullshit battles on their behalf, those fucking cowards, those fucking kids their damn selves.

I laid there shuddering in my narrow-ass bed, which would normally mean January, or Chicago's worstfuckingmonththankgodits-theshortest February. But not tonight. Something in the air was different. The whole house was asleep, and it was late in the summer and still pretty warm. My ma in their room down the hallway by the front door and just past the little room my two sisters shared. Me and my brother had beds jammed in the enclosed back porch of a typical North Side six-flat, the kind that was painted grey, smelled like piss, and had a redneck landlady's son that lived in the basement, who sold tic and weed and pulled the legs off cats, plus wore aviator sunglasses day and night and a leather jacket, no shirt. The light from the moon was huge, and the disc in the sky even bigger, like it had been sitting in the alley right behind the garage all day, just waiting for it to turn dark and now here it was, just outside our window. I thought about reaching my hand out and touching it, but that kind of gesture isn't for kids like you and me, is it?

I got out of bed and walked the three or four steps to the kitchen. The back door was to the right, with the chain pulled across all set and the yellowy, curling ripped shade hanging most of the way down. The little light on the stove was on, and I could see the ashtray piled with butts. I listened down the pitch-black hallway for a minute, and when no noises came back, I picked out a good-sized half one and lit it off the stove like my ma always did. I knew this was one of hers because the old man smoked his almost down to the filter, and those only had a drag or two left, the cheapskate son of a bitch. Man was he ever happy when Old Golds got labeled as generics, their unexpected price drop the only dividend he ever really got.

I sat at the kitchen table and smoked that cigarette, no shirt on but wearing the pants I usually slept in, since you never knew when you might have to take off. My leg started to trot, and I listened to the clock on the wall click along while I picked at the gold flecks in the Formica on the tabletop, the ones that would never come off, never fade. I don't know what I thought about that night, at that moment, but I really wish I did now. What's it like to have seventy or eighty years ahead of you, and what does your mind consider when it thinks it only has twenty or so at the most? What is the weight of the just-woke mind, the heft of a world limited on one plane by circumstance and venal authority but known on another that it's been tricked and lied to, that so much more awaits?

I jumped at a noise down at the bottom of the backstairs. It sounded like somebody cracked their shin on one of the wooden steps because the aftermath had more f-words and "cocksuckers" than a pirate galley, and that could only mean one thing.

The old man was home.

Son of a bitch.

I quick-stubbed out my smoke and tiptoed back to the porch and hopped in my bed, my toes quickscaling down the sheet I pulled up, tiny lightning storms of static electricity popping where my skin made the circuit with the fabric. I hupped up my feet so the sheet went under and then I pulled it up tight to my chin and shoved my hands behind my butt. I couldn't cover my face with a sheet or a blanket, though, because in my mind that would make me dead, and I wasn't ready to go just yet. I puffed my long hair off my face with a quick blow up from my lips then closed my right eye, the one on the doorway side, and rolled my left around, trying to guess what was about to happen.

The old man made it up to our place on the second floor after a while, after lots of swearing and tearing, and rustling, and stops for drinks from a tall boy, or a half-pint, whatever he had left from drinking on the El on the way home, the train trying to clack him to sleep but probably just irritating the shit out of him. I could even hear him say a muffly "godDAMmit" when I know he burned the insides of two fingers trying to pull a cigarette away from his lips where it had stuck so he could tip the ash that got too long but for which he was too drunk to "pppffffhhh" blow away without taking it out of his mouth. The double blisters you get when that happens are a real bitch because the bubbles just rub at each other until you pop them. After that, it takes forever for them to heal.

Once he got to the back door, though, shit got real—real quick. He finally got his key in the lock, sure, but the door wouldn't open because

the chain.

Shit.

The chain was on the door. Ma must've got pissed waiting for him to come home and put the chain on. And I walked right by it, didn't even think about it.

Fuck.

And now, he was pissed.

He started trying to sweet talk his way inside. He recounted his love, his devotion, and then his need, his desire. We heard about his job, and his family-man style, his not missing work, his dedication to his career, his drive to make something nice in this world.

Silence from the darkened hallway where their bedroom was.

He called on that one god and his son, Jesus. Mary. Joseph. Josephine and Mary Josephine, our grandmas, especially "Unnamed Ojibway woman" and then our ancestors, even the grandfathers, his drunken breath and oaths leaning in through the gap in the door. And though it was alcohol strong, it couldn't move or melt the chain that denied him access to our apartment, the sanctuary and the hearth, but more likely the bed that he so desperately needed, the one he should've been in so he could sleep the sleep of the imagined just, or at least the drunk, since that one part, that was no lie—he was utterly dedicated to work and never missed a day, except when he was in jail for another story entirely, because, I think, in the end, that work is what paid for what he really wanted to do, for the thing he felt he was born for; that job and that devotion paid for him to drink.

But on this night, he thought of someone besides himself, and that someone was my mother. Like all good addicts, to him, the fact that he had thought of someone other than himself should be somehow noted by the cosmos, that big, beautiful moon, I suppose, should have escorted him up into the night sky to rest among the stars, I suppose, because the old man had brought home

ARTHUR FUCKING TREACHER'S

you bitch

I got
ARTHUR FUCKING TREACHER'S
I got hushpuppies
and
I got shrimps
and
I got
ARTHUR FUCKING TREACHER'S
so
OPEN THE FUCKING DOOR RIGHT NOW
or
I WILL FUCKING KILL YOU.
And then the glass broke under the force of his fist, the bale of
his ire, and the fire of his drink. First try, first pop, right through
the vintage pane.
He fumbled with the chain.
Both of my eyes were open now, and rolling.
I could hear him trying to open the door, closing and opening it,
fiddling with the chain
and
I couldn't not help my dad
and so I
walked the three or four steps to the kitchen
and saw a lunatic,
a decoupage Indian Orthodox icon of sadness
and despair
and love,
and sour-fogged soul, and much nose breathing, and handfuls
of greasy brown paper, malt vinegar spilling over the broken glass
and the shattered wood, mixing its tang with the peppery copper
smell of the red sliding down the heavy milk-white painted back
door, sprays of drops and pinpoints everywhere and his black hair

hanging down over his five-hundred-year-old eyes that know how this is all going to turn out, how it would always turn out, no matter the prayers, no matter the hope and

then the bedroom door in the hallway burst open

just as he broke through and snapped the chain

and my ma took her self alone

and ran out the front door

into the night

lord knows where

her nightgown flashing through the present and into a past where just maybe she could rewrite all that had happened here

and where maybe next time

we'd get a bigger piece of things, a better slice of all we ever deserved, those little bits that get taken for granted dusted across the top of a better morning, one not mourning all this shit tonight.

9. ORACLE

Capitalism is the legitimate racket of the ruling class.

—ALPHONSE GABRIEL CAPONE

aux Moorish and French Revival architecture used to dot Chicago like sugar ants on a dropped Bomb Pop. Those sites, those temples of carving and fresco were dedicated to the Seventh Art in beautiful ways. The Grenada, Uptown, Riviera, Avalon, and others, those palaces that showed second-run movies for cheap were a wondrous sight, a weekly dose of magic in our grey and asphalt lives, holding moments we wouldn't appreciate for years. The Adelphi, our neighborhood theater, was a little older but had received an Art Deco update that put in chaise lounges and multicolored glass-rod lighting and terrazzo and mosaic tiling with giant ushers who had the one big eye of Alex in the pop-modern movie poster of *A Clockwork Orange* inlayed right on the sidewalk in black, white, and maroon. Your thirteen-year old self paid a buck and walked into any R- or X-rated movie you wanted.

One Friday, one of those R-rated movies was *Halloween*. We weren't about to miss it.

The problem was the dollar to get in. I didn't have any money. Jimmy1, he had money, sometimes Jimmy2 was cashy, Jimmy3 never, and Mickey, always. He used to steal money out of his uncle's pants—Paul, the bachelor off the boat from Ireland who lived with Mickey and his family. Every day he'd be drunk enough by five to forget where he was and by nine couldn't remember his name, let alone how much money he had left. He'd stumble home on autopilot by ten and pass out, pants on a chair by the door. After Da holy-watered the house and it was time for everyone to go to bed, Mickey would head into Paul's room and come out ten or twenty or sometimes fifty bucks the richer.

I envied and pitied his game. I mean, really. That's your family, man.

But this week's movie was *Halloween*. Sure, we were going to the show no matter what. We saw *Xanadu* and *The Exorcist*, *I Spit on Your Grave* and *The Best Little Whorehouse in Texas*, *Star Wars* and *The Kentucky Fried Movie*. In the movies we got to inhabit a demimonde, alone in the dark, descending into our fears and desires, ascending to their screen-lit exhibition. It never really mattered what was playing, but *Halloween* was something we were pretty psyched to see. So yeah. I had to come up with the dough.

Sometimes I would bet the other kids in my class on my Friday test score. I would go to class maybe once a week, sometimes twice, and I'd bet all these folks from the West Side I'd get a hundred on the test. They were like, "Dang, man. You never even come to class. No way." I didn't have the scratch to cover the bet, but I knew my abilities. Shiiiit. I had read all these textbooks two or five times in detentions. Wasn't nothing hard to remember in any of them. The teacher was cool, told the class I was "autodidactic." I think they thought I was an LD, had a learning disability or something. But whatever, I was happy to take their money. I could scratch out some change here and there lagging quarters out on the sidewalk, sometimes bus tokens, but the real money was in betting on tests. Man. Even after I got a little older I used to bet on *Jeopardy!* in the bars down by the Chicago Board of Trade, drinking all night for free on my winnings. When you look like me, people think you're dumb. And that shit pays.

But this week there was no test. And I was broke.

That meant it was time to drift west, head out to those sleepier neighborhoods, the ones where they kept their returnable bottles on the back porch. All you had to do was cut school and start walking toward where people worked all day. Those grey-enameled backstairs on every three flat on the North Side of Chicago were goldmines of pop bottles back in the day. We'd grab up a grocery cart and head down the alleys, scoping out people's stashes. We didn't really have to worry about cops or truant officers out this way. Man, we pulled all kinds of shit out this way. I remember this one time when

me and Frankie and Jimmy3 were down on Clark Street on a Thursday night, broke as fuck and just wanting to get high or something, anything. It was deep summer, you know, when it's like eighty-eight degrees at midnight, so muggy all the streetlights have rainbows around them and it's hard to hear the bus coming down the street. People talk when they walk by, but it sounds like they have scarves wrapped around their faces and the words they're saying aren't for you anyway, and they act like you aren't even there while they secretly hope they're escaping your gaze. I couldn't take it anymore, and Jimmy and Frankie were bored, talking shit, kicking at garbage cans and looking deep in at store windows. I figured we should do something.

"Hey. Let's get the fuck out of here," I said. "Go west."

"Yeah, sure, Teddy. What do you want to do?" Frankie asked.

"I don't know, man. Just not this."

"I hear you, Folks," Jimmy mumbled. "Let's fucking go, bro."

"Aight, let's do it, Folks," I agreed.

"Coo'," Frankie smiled, and we headed out.

We walked on, shirtless, through alleys nominally known, baggies clinging in the heat and humidity, sharing the last of a 40 ounce Mickey's Malt Liquor, stopping to tag 𝕾𝕮ℝ / 𝕾imon 𝕮ity ℝoyals with a big black Magnum marker wherever it would fit—glass grocery-store window, car hood, newspaper box, or house front door, it didn't matter. We turned off the main street after a while, walking into the neighborhood. Frankie spoke up after we went a block or so.

"Let's do it, Folks."

"Do what?" I asked.

"Yeah, what, Folks?" Jimmy added in.

"This crib, Folks," Frankie pointed.

"What?" I said, eyes flicking to each window, looking for lights and Beware of Dog signs, then back to the streetlights and the silent rows of town homes.

"This crib," he repeated.

"What you want to do?" Jimmy asked.

"I'm going in." Frankie's eyes lit up and he grinned big.

"Nah, man. Let's do a grocery store or something." With one eye I could see the blue light from a TV through one of the windows. With the other, I could see Frankie digging in his pants.

"Just got this, homes. Checkitout." Frankie held up a little chrome .25 for us to see.

"You ain't even," I said. "Not for a burglary."

"Well, we'll see if he's gonna make it a burglary or a home invasion."

"Damn, homes. Why you tryna make it a felony—"

"*I* ain't tryna make it *shit*, bro. That's up to him."

Jimmy laughed, still high as a kite on those dummy sticks he liked, said, "I'll go."

"Nah," Frankie shook his head. "I'll be right out."

Cicadas droned. It was foggier out this way, wetter. They had trees and shit.

"Aight, Folks. What you want us to do?" I said.

"Just keep a eye out, bro. I'll be right back." Frankie walked off.

I side-eyed him a little as he went in through the back door and wondered if he had only seen in the papers about us getting a reputation for home invasions and then decided he was the one making that rep when he came out five minutes later with a VCR and a pickle jar full of change and I remembered he couldn't read.

"Shit, homes," I laughed. What else could I do?

Jimmy laughed too. "Gimme that change, bro," he said.

"Fuck you, man. I did all the work," Frankie crabbed.

"Let's get the fuck out of here," I said.

We cruised up the nearest alley behind the Centrella, cut right through the next street and into its alley then headed farther west. I took a leak, and Jimmy tagged the shit out of a garage. They had those out this way. So much empty canvas . . .

"Leave it, homes," Frankie hissed at him.

"What, bro?" Jimmy said.

"Let's *go.*" Frankie waved his hand.

I wondered what was next. His ardently criminal mind, once engaged, was extremely capable.

"I want to do that one laundromat," he continued.

"Which one?" I asked.

"You know, the one on Touhy Ave."

"Shit. It's right on the main street, bro."

"What are you, some kind of pussy? I thought you were our warlord," Frankie shot back.

"I am, bitch. I'm also in charge of keeping your ass out of jail," I said.

"We ain't going to no jail out here, Midget," he laughed. "They don't even have cops out this way," he added.

"You're right about that, homes," I agreed.

"Let's do it," Jimmy perked up.

"Alright." I looked up and down the street toward Touhy. All quiet. "Let's do it," I said.

"Hit it, Folks," Frankie nodded, and off we went.

It was mid-late summer, four o'clock in the morning, seventy-two degrees with 95 percent humidity and no breeze. We made our way down the alley west of Western Avenue off Touhy, part of Chicago that's ethnic and suburban at the same time, city but not city. Places still leave their early-morning bakery out on the street and don't worry about thieving. Quiet and foggy in all kinds of ways. We headed west, bad intentions and unsure hearts committed to things we shouldn't but have no say in, really, our fates predetermined by structures beyond our control. We vaguely knew this, and still decided to have a good time.

We rolled up on the back side of the laundromat on the avenue. We were apprehensive but giddy without even knowing why. *BAM*, we kicked in the back door. Blue from the streetlights out front glowed across the counters, and we scrambled like we'd never done this before, but Frankie found the cashbox like he had a map. Sixteen pounds of quarters, dimes, and nickels in a little laundry bag, plus a stack of bills for the next day's bank. We got our asses out of Dodge and down Rockwell toward Indian Boundary Park.

Once we were deep inside and near the big pond, we divvied it up. I got around fifty-six dollars, thought about the trade of three to five for that one, marveled at the depth of cheapness I'd just accepted for the value of my life. At precisely 4:45 a.m., I wondered who in the hell will accept nickels and quarters by the ounce for payment.

At 4:46 I decided

I don't give a fuck.

Money is money. I'm super sick of class shit I'm not even aware of yet.

Just so you know, it's super satisfying to order ham and eggs and pancakes and pay for all that noise with nickels. It just is. You tip out in bills but give the owners nickels. Fuck 'em. It's for all those times they wouldn't wait on you, stared you down, made you feel like shit in your own country, your own hood, your own rez. Yeah. Fuck you, grown-ups. Eat shit.

Have a nice day, assholes. Tonight's the night he comes home.

10. WHEN TWO TRIBES GO TO WAR

Hahahahaha!

—JIMMY3

"**H**ey Teddy," Jimmy2 says. "Did you go see Frankie in Joliet?"

"Yeah. Last week. Where the fuck you been?" We're sitting on the couch in his ma and stepdad's apartment off Damen Avenue near Fargo, North Side Chicago. I like this place okay, I guess. I got a real thing with other people's houses, their blue-velour couches and the sad seashells full of hand soaps you're not allowed to use, ditto the weird things they call "hand towels." But they both work, are never home, and have an air conditioner. Today at ten in the morning it's already hot as shit outside.

"Well I know you seen him, man. I'm just trying to make conversation."

I wasn't really in the mood for small talk. People were getting on my nerves, and I was spending way too much time in my head. Example, I woke up this morning with an itch on my soul, and all I can think about is how we all die slow, but some of us just enjoy it more than others. What the fuck is that. I'm a kid, man. I hate having to start drinking when the sun is just coming over the roof line. It fucks with my light and mood all day. I'm still trying to work through how I'm still young enough that I can consume, rather than be consumed by, love. Or some bullshit like that. Death can wait.

"Make conversation? You been watching soap operas with Lena again, ain't it?"

"No. I was just—"

"Bullshit, man. But it's okay—"

"No, for real."

"Fine, man. What the fuck do I care? Let's converse, then."

"Fuck you, Teddy. You're such an asshole."

"Yeah, I know," I say. "I'm trying to make it my trademark."

He sulks. Goes into his bedroom and comes back with his boombox. Puts on Tom Petty.

"Are you kidding me with that shit? I fuckin' hate Tom Petty."

"Fuck you. This is a great album."

"No it isn't. He sucks. His voice sounds like Bob Dylan trying to fuck a duck."

"Fine. What do you want to hear?"

"The Clash."

"Oh, really?"

"Yeah. Put it on."

"Okay."

Jeezus. Was that so hard I think? We listen to London Calling. I'm just pissy, so I say,

"Wanna hear a Frankie story?"

"Sure," Jimmy2 says. "Tell me a fuckin' story then," and he pops the tape out.

"Alright. Where's your brother's bong?"

"He'll kill us," Jimmy2 says.

"Nah, man. It'll be alright—"

"Fuck that, Teddy man. He'll be pissed off."

"It's under the couch, ain't it? Get it out." I reach under the cream-colored couch with the rust and black floral pattern, past some old popcorn, a dildo I think, a pair of shorts, and some cheerios. Ah, there it is. A purpley-colored graphic. Nice.

"Put some water in this. Or apple juice. You got any apple juice?"

"Nah. How about V8?"

"What the fuck. It's about the *flavor*, not the fact it's juice."

"Oh. Okay. I think we got grape juice."

"Better water it down then," I say. "That's gonna be too strong."

"Okay," he says. "I'll be right back."

He stomps off toward the kitchen. I look at the giant console TV. Whaddup, Bob Barker, my Rosebud pal, Sicangu Lakota gameshow host? The clicker is right there, but man I love *The Price is Right*. It's the one game with the yodeling and shit right now though, so I get up and turn the sound down.

Jimmy2 comes back with the bong all freshened up, purple juice sloshing in the even more purple acrylic. I pull out a tiny twist of weed in some saran wrap.

"Let me see that," I say.

"Here." He hands me the bong.

I pinch into the bowl, dump the shake out into my hand, and pack the rest. I'm not a huge fan of weed, but some days . . .

"Here," I say. "Your crib, your hit. You can do the first one."

He pulls out a lighter and hits the bowl. A seed pops and the ember lands in his hair.

I laugh. "Your hair is on fire, man."

"What the fuck!?" he slaps at the top of his head, smoke rolling out of his mouth while he starts coughing. Well he's gonna be blowed, I think, smile.

"Let me see that," I say, pull out my own lighter and brick a huge hit, pulling the carb when the tube is pure white. I hold it so long hardly any smoke comes out at all. I throw my head back and let a few whisps leak up.

Jimmy2 scrapes away at the bowl, pulls another hit.

Before we know it, it's the Showcase Showdown. Ceramic Dalmatians and a K-Car. Hahaha. Who would want this shit?

"You know what?" I say.

"No. What?" Jimmy2 asks.

Frankie had no idea how far they'd gone. But as he looked through the passenger window, that one part of his mind that had some order to it counted the telephone poles, kept a running total. He asked it how many poles and told it to keep up. Cause once he knew, all he had to do was look up the standard distance between rural telephone poles and then knock out a little multiplication, one of the few parts of the GED math section he could pass, but since he kept flunking the rest he stopped taking it, even when it meant he had to finish out a six-month stay in his local level 3 working in the kitchen. Probably about three hundred feet apart out here in the sticks, he figured. If he doubled that, it would at least tell him about how far away they were from the last shithole town that didn't even have a liquor store to rob. Goddamn Baptists. He counted for a while, looking out at the marching red cedar poles, and beyond them the windmills like giants doing lazy toe touches, the endless plains calling to him. They swayed and whispered to roll down the window, look deep into the distance across the far field, the sun gold-redding his face, the sky lit from within, its own soul of bright just above the ridgeline, halfway to the top of this most perfect picture ever, and he reached out to it, beyond the door, and he grabbed wind by the armfuls, trying to take its cleanse home with him.

Home wasn't anywhere for right now, probably the three weeks in the front passenger side of this '74 Monte Carlo the longest he had lived anywhere in a long time. Him and Jimmy had bought it on a lot in Altus, Oklahoma, at some dumpy dealership on Main Street. He had used the car lot's shitter in a yellow brick outbuilding that introduced him to those little black scorpions that were always almost as angry as his ma. He laughed big and loud like a donkey when one of them kept trying to kill him through his heavy work boots until he just stepped on it, but still. Jesus Christ. What a fucking plague.

The maroon two-door heap of shit had a leaky radiator, so they had to do a lot of jerking the wheel from side to side to slosh the water around while driving and dumping pepper packs in it from truck stops and gas stations and refills from the sides of deserted-looking house spigots to keep it from overheating, and it cost them four hundred bucks and a bag of ditchweed the redneck salesman insisted they had because of their long hair and whatnot and he was right but still anyway, and it had the 454 V-8 Turbo-Jet Hydra-Fucking-Matic so he wouldn't have given a shit if he had to lean out the window and blow on the motor wherever they went. They bought it. It was time to leave town anyway. They'd been here about a week, and that was eight days too long by his reckoning. It was early May, and there'd been a snowstorm; hail the size of golf balls; two tornados; and three days of a hundred degrees with two hundred percent humidity. No fucking wonder they gave this place to us Indians, he thought.

Besides, they were cashy, had about nine hundred dollars and a bottle of what looked like Lemon 714s they took off some crew-cutted shitbird they met at the VFW who dealt crappy meth and even dirtier coke to the airmen from the base. He was all talking about being a King, an LK, Peoples out here in the middle of nowhere's asshole. Had a stick-and-poke jailhouse crown on his forearm. Frankie aimed to cut that fucker out of there at some point. King Killer, Queen Thriller. Royal Love, peckerwood.

This drive was getting to be a real drag. He'd never been so hungry. What the fuck. And there was never anywhere to eat out here. He missed those Whataburger places, and Blake's felt a million miles away. He thought maybe they were in Kansas by now, maybe Nebraska, but it could've been South Dakota for all he knew. They were headed north, but his geography skills were way worse than his half-ass math chops.

Jimmy wasn't saying much. He was kind of pussing out after they rolled that dealer. What was his name, the skinny-ass motherfucker? Cheech, Chuy, nah, Chuckie. He wore baggies like they did, a white dago tee, black suede rocker-bottom shoes. He had a weird crew-cut thing going, but whatever, when in Rome they guessed. Since Frankie was Native and Jimmy was black, they told this Chuckie fuck they were UnKnowns (the only other mixed set besides Royals) from up in Chicago when they met him at the VFW. Frankie and Jimmy had walked into the men's room, checking the place out. Chuckie had just sold a light quarter to some E-3 looking kid (mustache, no beard) for forty bucks. Jesus. What a racket. Frankie thought if he could stand the hell-on-earth weather and the dogshit food he'd make a pile of dough here, but there was no way he could stomach the trade.

They looked at him and said,

Hey, what's up, man? Starting at his hands and looking up and down for tattoos, seeing a crown on his left arm.

Ain't nothin', the scrawny dealer said.

What you ride, man? Frankie said.

King Love, homes. Five poppin' six droppin', the Corona talked shit.

Hmmm, Jimmy said.

UK all the way, Frankie said.

We're UnKnowns, bro. Halsted and Wrightwood, he finished.

Montrose and Hazel Kings, Chuckie said.

Alright peoples, Jimmy said.

They said
I'm Jimmy
and
I'm Frankie.
Cool,
I'm Chuckie, the Latin King said.

They headed over to the bar, made fun of the way the white girls danced, glared at the white boys, drank Modelos or Millers, whatever, got Chuckie to do a couple shots of Cuervo. Everyone was feeling good. They even did a couple lines of Chuckie's shitty blow. Frankie watched Chuckie. A lot. Set his mouth, chewed the inside of his bottom lip. Chuckie didn't notice, but Jimmy did. He chugged his beer and shuddered.

Hey. Let's get the fuck out of here, Frankie said.

For sure, peoples. Let's go, Chuckie said.

They got to Chuckie's door-slapping trailer, pushed some fly strips out of the way, and walked inside.

Frankie smashed in the back of Chuckie's head with a golf club he found who the fuck knows where, a five-iron, right there in the kitchen. Chuckie crashed face first on the yellow and white linoleum floor, his blood landing in a fine spray pattern around his head milliseconds later. But he was awake, his eyes rolling around, looking at his shitty appliances from an angle he'd probably never seen, never considered before. Jimmy pulled up a chair at the kitchen table, opened a beer, a Modelo or a Miller, lit a smoke.

Frankie laughed that jackass laugh of his and rolled Chuckie over. The little dealer tried to talk, but Frankie put his hand over his mouth and shushed him. He took out a grubby pocketknife, plunged it into the middle of that five-pointed crown, then dragged across and started to cut a circle around it. Blood sparkly and bright jetted up. Frankie took his hand off Chuckie's mouth so he could use his fingers to spread the skin on his arm, make a cleaner cut. Chuckie made a weird noise, but he didn't scream, didn't cuss, nothing, eyes just looking somewhere over Frankie's shoulder.

Frankie sawed away, pulled the crown off, and stuck it on the refrigerator like a blue-starred homework assignment. Chuckie gagged. Jimmy laughed and ground his smoke into the kitchen floor. Frankie noticed he had cut his hand in the crotch of his thumb while working on Chuckie. He took two steps over to the sink to wash the cut out, already gross and looking infected. He swiveled to admire his work on the fridge one more time and then walked over, punched the dealer in the face, knocked him out, and dried his hands on Chuckie's dago tee. Chuckie was passed the fuck out, with the faintest smile on his face. Frankie went through his pockets, grabbed his roll of cash, a couple of pill bottles besides the 'luudes on the counter (Praziquantel? Lomitil? What the hell are those?), and his keys—just to be a dick, Jimmy guessed. They turned out the lights and left.

And now here they were in the middle of who knows where, light glinting off the hood of that '74 Monte Carlo, Jimmy jerking it side to side, the heat blasting to keep the motor cool. Driving in silence since they were afraid to put on the radio because you know you need to listen for any potential automotive death throes.

Little black tentacles whipped around inside Frankie's irises as he stared over at Jimmy, the red red sunlight outlining the tiny sucker pads, sweat rolling down his forehead.

Frankie said, Pull over, man. I'm hungry.

So hungry.

"You're such a fucking liar, man."

"We're all fucking liars, Jimmy."

11. THE PROPHET AT THE WOODEN NICKEL

No red man must ever drink liquor, or he will go and have
the hot lead poured in his mouth!

—TENSKWATAWA, *THE OPEN DOOR*

Me and the Prophet survey the bar on down from the entryway. Two of my Indian-way uncles are arguing about movie stars. My pop is passed out at the end of the bar, skinny ass gripped tight to the stool, assuredly going nowhere, head down in a puddle of ash, warm beer, and glass sweat, snoring away the breath of the righteously drunk, moving into another world. The jukebox plays Patsy Cline almost not loud enough to hear, but I know that's "Crazy" tinkling through all the conversations. The Christmas lights are still up, always up, just how I like them. Beer signs sizzle and crack in the dark room and people talk words in their glow.

The Open Door turns to me and asks, Is it always this way?

I look him up and down, his shape shimmering in the smoke haze, his face in and out like a black and white Zenith that's lost its tinfoil rabbit ears.

"It's always been this way, at least for me," I say.

Hmmm, he says.

"Frank," I say to the bartender, walking over toward the taps. "Can I get some caramel corn? Put it on the old man's tab?"

"Sure thing, Speedy," he says, reaches back to the rack of chips and shit, hands me the mostly clear bag with the navy-on-white Jay's logo at the top.

Frank is either twenty or a hundred and fifty years old, I can never tell. He's from White Earth. I think he's related to my godparents, but either way, he treats me like a nephew / little brother, so he's the goods in my book.

The Prophet leans in, asks me what I just got.

"Caramel corn."

What is that? He asks.

"I think you would've called it maize or something." Visions of that chick in the commercials flash in my head. "But it's like tossed in cooked sugar," I say.

Does that make alcohol? He asks.

"No. Just cooked, syrupy, like with maple, yeah?" I say.

Hmmm, he says.

I know he couldn't taste it even if he wanted to, so I say, "It's so sweet it hurts your teeth just to eat it. You probably wouldn't like it. It's kinda for kids."

Probably good, though, yeah?

"Yup. It is, but too much will make you sick," I say.

As in a serious illness? Why would you eat that?

"No. Just sick to your stomach," I say.

Then you better not eat too much, he says.

"I won't, Tenskwatawa. I won't."

Is that your father there? He asks.

"That's him," I say.

He's liquor sick, isn't he? the Prophet asks.

"I think so," I say. "I think if you mean not beating us up too much, keeping the lights on and cooking one meal a week he's liquor sick, but maybe not terminally, sure. He's sick alright."

A father should never beat his children, the Prophet says.

"Times have changed, Grandfather," I say. "Maybe sometimes we do things that make us deserve it."

Never, he says. Never do children deserve to be beaten.

"I'll remember that," I say.

You would do well to, he says.

I've never forgotten.

"But Wayne Newton isn't a fucking Indian," says Leksi Tommy, his fattened Oglala face earnestly pleading his case, with an edge.

"The fuck he isn't," Leksi Joe replies, matching that edge, his mean Sicangu eyebrows flaring like his big nostrils. "I know he sings that German song, but he's an Indian, goddamit."

"Bullshit. And if he is," snorts Tommy, "he's a fuckin' Cherokee."

"Ha. You're the dumbass who told me Anthony Quinn was an Indian. Cause he played Flapping Eagle and visited Alcatraz? Sheeeit. He played a better Eskimo than any of that fake Indian shit and he was in a movie called *Never Love a Drunken Indian*. I'm a drunken Indian. Fuck that guy. You're an idiot. Wayne Newton is some Virginia tribe anyway. And you know Teddy Sr.'s ex-old lady was a Cherokee. You need to knock that shit off before he wakes up and hears you. Plus, his kid is right there. What if that was his mom you were talking about? She could've been."

"His real mom *is* a Cherokee," Joe says.

"No she isn't. She might be part hásapa, but she ain't Indian."

"Fuckin' ayyy, Tommy, you're a real asshole."

Tenskwatawa says, are these two your uncles?

"Yup," I say.

This is what liquor does to people, he says. They sound like idiots, like white men.

"It's a white man thing, so that makes sense, I guess," I offer.

Mmmhmmm, he says. They are impugning your mother's honor. I don't know your language, but this hásapa word doesn't sound like a compliment.

"It's not, really, at least not the way they're using it," I say. "But they're drunk."

You know if my brother was here, things would not go well for these two.

"I know," I say. "If I see him later, maybe I'll ask him for some advice."

I think we both know what that would be, he says.

"It's alright," I say. "They don't mean anything by it."

But they do, he says. Or else they wouldn't say it.

"It's okay. Don't worry about it."

Okay. Is that an Indian word? It sounds like something Choctaws might use.

"It sounds like it, but it's not. I think it comes from the Americans. But it means everything is alright, in any case," I say.

Okay, he says, watching the word come out of his mouth, drift across the bar.

"Okay," I say, thinking he's right. It doesn't sound English at all.

"Maybe I am. But what about Ricardo Montalban? He's definitely an Indian," Tommy says.

"Holy shit. This guy," Joe says.

"Eeeez. You know I'm right," says Tommy.

"Because he played a Blackfeet named Iron Shirt? Fuck him and fuck them, too," says Joe.

"This one. Eeeez," says Tommy again. "What about Elvis?"

"Everyone knows Elvis is an Indian."

"Alright, den."

"Flaming Star, Stay Away Joe? Sheeeit. Elvis is a fuckin' Indian," says Joe.

"Okay, man. Calm down."

They drink in silence for a while. Marty Robbins tells us about his adventures in Texas. Tenskwatawa flickers in and out. I eat caramel corn and peek at my dad, who snores away.

"Hey Joe," Tommy says, peeling the label off his Schlitz.

"What, asshole?" Joe replies, looking over the top of his heavy black frames, trying to fill his glass from his pitcher and what's left of someone else's, working hard to keep a cigarette butt from bouncing over the lip and into his drink.

Tommy says, "This Oglala and this Rosebudder were driving out of Pine Ridge and they stopped at the White River to take a piss."

"Yeah?"

"Yeah. So they get out of the truck and head over to the bridge and they're standing there pissing and the Rosebudder goes, 'Eeee this water is cold, init?'"

Joe laughs. "That's right, fucker!"

Tommy continues,

"And the Oglala goes, 'Shit, it's deep, too.'"

"Hahahahahaha!"

"Hahahahahaha!"

"Good one, Tommy, you motherfucker!"

"Hahaha, Joe. Gotcha!"

"Ayyy. Buy me a drink, Mr. Big Dick!"

"Okay, misun. I got you."

Tenskwatawa shakes his head at me, eyes not leaving my face.

"At least they're having fun. You can see they care about each other," I say.

Do they? Do they really?

I don't really have an answer for that, but I say, "Sure they do."

Okay, he says, the word sharp and blue, twisting for just a second in the dark air.

Okay.

Vassily is trying to quit smoking. I look over and that savage heathen has an upside-down cross of nicotine patches across his shaved and sweaty chest and stomach. He sees me counting them and laughs.

I'm trying to listen to a Hank Williams Sr. album and wondering why this Ukrainian linguist-turned-limo driver who keeps talking over it is my friend.

"This *music*, to Vassily, this *accompaniment* to bearded cousins making the sex act, this is not good," he says. "Picturing dirty overalls, and Red and Black Abners from Bugs Bunny pulling each other rotted teeth." Vassily likes to make air quotes when he emphasizes words.

Jesus, he was harsh. I felt lonely as Kaw-Liga when I woke up this afternoon, so yeah, I put this record on repeat and called Vassily. Thought that would be fine, but none of it was working. Hank turned overly plaintive, and Vassily turned prick.

It's hotter than hell outside. We're roasting in the "living" room of my shithole cold-water squat above an abandoned bowling alley on Belmont Avenue in Chicago and drinking shots of vodka from a full bottle I found in the back of the freezer. We'd been at it for a bit, but it was still too humid to get drunk, the liquor sweating out before our livers could wring the fun from it. Looking at the light, though, it was getting close to dark, the last bits of sun streaking out of the West Side to edge the windows and rooflines across the street in liquid gold foil and ambered glass, the shadows just purple and not yet black.

"You know that's Popov you're drinking there, asshole?" I say.

"What!? You fucker. Would give me the cheapest Polack vodka? Not even Sobieski? Why hate Vassily?"

I say, "Kidding. It's Smirnoff. Some Russian you are, ya—"

"Fuck you. Am *Ukrainian*, greasy red man. Do not make me tell story of Free Territory of Ukraine, 1919—"

"So I can one up you with fifty thousand years of anarcho-communism in this hemisphere? Don't do it, Vassily."

"Jesus, Fyodor. You are biggest asshole sometime."

"You got that right." I give him the twin finger guns. I want to launch into a lecture about the long Polish-Ukrainian Golden Age, but he's a recalcitrant prick *and* an unreconstructed 1950s-style communist, so fuck it.

We drink in silence for what seems like hours, Vassily thankfully not given over to the Western need to pointlessly fill the air with self-made sounds and nervous words. I smoke the occasional cigarette, watch the black of night tendril up the red bricks outside, the sky around the early-risen moon narrowing its lids around the yellowy eye of its nearly full face. When the antique blue and white neon of the Courtesy liquor store comes on I stub out my smoke and say,

"Vassily. Let's go out."

"Thank god, this fucker making me cry with smoking in here. Vassily miss smoking so much," he assures me, puppy-dog eyes and all, pulling on a grimy orange T-shirt.

"Man," I say. "You gotta be tripping with all those patches on you."

He yanks the shirt down over his rounded gut. "Just never mind. Anyway, Feo, these patches two days old."

"I thought you smelled a little ripe. Don't those come off in the shower?"

"*Shower* (air quotes), Mister Cold-Water Shithole? When last time you clean self?"

"Indians don't stink like you monkey-people do. We don't have that nasty peeled onion B.O."

"But are greasy enough slide through that rathole by hot plate in kitchen, so—"

"So fuck you, Vassily. Rat holes are like farms where you come from."

"Ha! At least having meat to eat, noodle king. All that ramen must make tapeworms feel right at home in Feo's underused bowels."

"Damn, Vassily. That's cold. Not as cold as your never-used other side of the bed in that flophouse you call 'home' (I return the air quotes), but yeah, sure."

"Do not fuck with me, Feo. Am full of terrible Polack vodka. Having belly full of potato-based fire and bad mood. Call truce."

"Truce, my friend," I say.

———

Friend (no air quotes). Men's friendships are fucked up. I mean, I'm glad for this younger generation, our kids, I suppose. They're doing it right, and for that I am grateful. They hug each other, genuinely ask each other how they're doing—hell, they even tell one another they care about each other. It's made it less awkward for our generation to be human while obligating us to be so, even if it's hard

86

sometimes. We grew up being unemotional and unloving, not showing our feelings, or being kind. Fuck, we couldn't even put sugar in our coffee. Now I cry at songs on the radio, when I read great lines in books, when the light in the sky is just right. It's fifty years of not saying or feeling jack shit poured into my adulthood, my fatherhood. It's a river of grief that appears at inopportune times, but it's also a joyful sadness I can share at least, tell to the folks who catalyze these grateful emotions into the world where they belong. And I don't have to feel shame about them. Yeah. That's okay to me. Real okay. But at this moment early in my twenties, me and Vassily are traditional men friends. That means we talk shit to each other constantly, never mention our love for one another, and beat the shit out of each other instead of hugging, unless we're super drunk. That last moment lives in the veil between those two worlds. I'm determined to head out and break on through.

"Let's fucking go, man!"

"Alright, alright, Feo. Are such prick sometimes."

"You know I like the near dark. Come on."

"Am coming. Having to piss now. Hold on."

"Fine." I light a smoke, lean back, tilt my face up, and lightly bang the back of my head against the plaster in the hall next to the front door. I can hear Vassily's urine assault the bowl through the thin wall of the bathroom. I really should move.

We head down the two stories of staircase to the street in the almost-black gloaming, what's left of the thin and spidery light leaking over the transom at the bottom of the stairwell. We jerk the door open, and a bum slo-mos over the threshold. "Never trust a junkie," he croaks, and we step around him onto the sidewalk, taking in the fresh air.

"Where going, Feo?" Vassily asks.

"To the Courtesy, my Uki friend," I reply.

"Jesus Christ," he shakes his head.

The Courtesy is a typical old-school neighborhood Chicago bar/liquor store. Old wooden bar on the right, coolers of to-go stuff on the left. It has a cadre of shitty wizened retirees possessed of Neanderthal politics and worry-worn coin purses, both evidence of solidly crappy educations and low-paying jobs, both serving their old-age needs, at least. Blowsy "broads" of similar age round out the color, and low-level weed and coke dealers fill in any cracks left open by the occasionally visiting offspring of the aforementioned elders. Things get ugly but never too violent while we watch Kojak reruns on Channel 9 with the sound turned off because we know every episode. It always closes on time (2:00 a.m.), its vaguely bewildered and simultaneously bored Korean owners rudely counting their money in front of their addled customers while future winos and their contemporary heroes try to buy road pops at less-than-inflated after-hours prices, which kick in at last call. Sometimes you can get a Tombstone pizza, but the oven behind the bar is usually broken, so it's Jay's O-ke-Doke cheese popcorn or Hot Stuff chips for dinner. I love and hate the place all at the same time, depending on my mood and capacity for self-reflection.

But tonight is different. The air inside and out hums with something that smells unusual, that curls around my cortex as I stand in the bathroom stall and do bumps off the corner of a book of matches, oblivious to the stink of missed opportunity around the toilet, wondering if I should share with Vassily, who though fading at his stool out there is a world-class hoover with no sense of propriety when it comes to coke and takes the this-might-be-our-last-night-on-earth approach to doing drugs, or drinking, or fighting, or fucking.

I walk out of the shitter and sure enough, I'm right. Two gangbangers with about thirty years between them are sticking the place up. They're waving crappy little automatics around, yelling in Spanglish to the Korean daughter to hand over the dinero. Her English is limited to serving shots and beers and her Spanish might get her a burrito with no crema, but that's about it. She's not too sure if they're joking or not, since they're so young they look like they should be hawking that shitty school music band chocolate instead of robbing liquor stores. She's ignoring them and no one else is really paying attention, Uncle Theo up on the little screen about to snake a sweet parking spot.

"¿Qué paso wey?!" I stupidly shout from the bathroom door, and promptly take a bullet to the leg.

"Mierda, mierda, mierda," they apologize in tandem, now realizing they're never going to make themselves understood unless they can find a gringo with a rudimentary understanding of Spanish to translate their larcenous plans.

It's gone through the meat on the side of my thigh. I reach back and realize it's a through and through, so I say, "Chevere, chevere. Está bien. Estaré bien. Qué paso wey?"

"¡Es un robo, pendejo!"

"Yeah, I figured that. Okay. Just relax," I say, holding up both hands, palms out. I look over at Vassily. He's passed out, head down, elbows up on the bar. No help there.

I tell the daughter very slowly, my hand held up with a trigger finger and cocked thumb, that these two are very bad guys, and they are robbing her family's place of business, that she needs to give them all the money in the register or (pulls trigger finger, makes pow! Sound) they will shoot and kill us all. She just started high school in America, so she gets this one quick. She takes up the bills in a pile, sets them on the bar, and then upends the drawer and starts to pour the change onto the counter. The clanging in the silence is deafening. Vassily wakes up and

out of nowhere pulls out this huge chrome revolver and starts blasting away.

One of the ceiling fans pangs and crashes down on the bar.

Kojak takes a shot to the lollipop, and the TV shatters dark and empty.

One of the Coronas gets grazed in the shoulder, and as he heads to the floor, he pulls off a shot that nicks the brim of his buddy's LA Kings hat and spins it off his head. Startled, his own .22 pops a cap into the open cooler, its only casualty the top of a St. Ides 40 ouncer that quietly leaks all over some Zimas in the bottom of the case. I grab the first kid's piece while he bitches about his arm going numb and tell the other one to drop his gun. Vassily is kinda hyperventilating while the daughter is grabbing up the bills. I try to blow my hair back off my forehead but no use and end up curling a bunch back behind my ear with one hand while my other holds the automatic out in front of me. I keep it steady on the two Kings while I walk over to the bar and grab my smokes, shake one out and light it, then flick my new pistol toward the door. I take a drag and go with "Vamanos, muchachos." They help each other out the door while the daughter yells about calling the police. I mumble something about "no harm no foul," but she's yelling and pointing at the ceiling fan. All the old folks go back to their drinks, and I jock the .32. Jesuscahrist. What a fuckin night. I talk the daughter into a complimentary twelve pack. I'm starving all of a sudden, but of course the Tombstone oven behind the bar is crapped out. Burritos it'll have to be. I grab up my brown paper bag of ree-wards along with Vassily and we head out down to Ashland Avenue for some carne asada, but not from the gringo pile. No cilantro, por favor. I wonder if I have any Vicodin at home for this leg, or at least some Tylenol 3s.

Twenty minutes later we're heading up the stairwell to my crib and I hug him like my whole life has depended on it.

I can hear him smile in the dark.

13. GYROS AND GAYLORDS

I don't want to be murdered beside the garbage cans
in some Chicago alley.

—ADELARD CUNIN (BUGS MORAN)

got sent to Lane Tech Home of the Indians High School. At
Addison and Western, it was, maybe still is, the second-largest
high school in Chicago, right behind CVS. That's Chicago
Vocational School, not the viral cut-rate dope dealers with the
eighty-eight-cent two liters of generic pop and the place to buy stale
Whitman's for all your last-minute Valentine's / Anniversary /
Mother's Day shit. The other school close by was Gordon Tech.
I think Styx played their prom once when they first started out.
And that was a Catholic school, so it was full of them and the
better-off kids from my grammar school. Whatever. This one time
in the back of the bus I watched some of their seniors grab this
Timmy kid, fresh off the boat from Ireland, turn him upside down,
and tie his shoelaces together over the hand-holding bar up top.
Every time the driver pulled into traffic or cut a sharp lane change,

Timmy and his big red Irish head would swing into the empty seats, and he would go "Owowow, woe and begorrah" or some shit like that, sounding like the Lucky Charms guy, but the side of his face was getting more purple-blue-green by the mile. The bus driver finally stopped laughing and came back to cut him down with a pocketknife.

Lane was on the edge of Gaylord territory, so there weren't all that many of them, but there were enough. The nearest rival public high school was Schurz, and it was crawling with them, but it was a ways away. I still remember the day a bunch of Lane football players walked through the cafeteria with purple Schurz jackets they probably ganked off some hapless freshmen, each with the bright gold *H* and *R* cut out so the backs read "SCUZ" in big block letters, remembered it at the time at least a little better than I remembered the school was named for Carl C. Fuckin' Schurz, the kraut piece of shit who was of course known for his civil-rights and reformer crapola, but forgotten for his reservation, relocation, and assimilation policies. So yeah. No one gives a shit about Indians, so fuck everybody all the way around, I guess.

I was late to school one day. Well, late for detention. *Before School Detention.* Just cruel. Got off the Western Avenue bus to no one around. Shit. Class had already started. I lived all the way up near Howard and Damen and had to get to Addison on one Howard Street and two Western Ave buses. It's a haul. Map it out some time. At 7:50 a.m. At thirteen years old. At a school I didn't want to go to, one that exactly none of my friends were at. One that gave me detention on the second day for being late. I didn't even know what that was, so I missed it, and got some more. That's why I had to get here today on time. Fuck.

I had already missed zero period, so I lit a smoke and walked around for a while. Periods were fifty minutes, so I had some time to kill. I sat on the sidewalk by the sub shop, which still wasn't open. I looked at my history book, but I had already read it when I was in fifth grade. I had like forty pages left in *The Silmarillion*, so I finished that. I grabbed my books, stood up, and lit another smoke. Flicked the match in front of me looking west on Addison and as it came down my eyes rack focused on a scrawny white boy wearing light-blue baggies and a white dago tee. Construction boots, dirty-ass hair, zits, and the eight-haired hint of a mustache that will never look quite right, no matter how long he grows it, that definitely will never be groomed. I could see the outline of a pack of smokes over his chest, straining against his shirt. It was about sixty-two degrees and cloudy.

A Gaylord.

Son of a bitch. Well alright, I thought. This'll kill a little time. I'm not gonna be hearing the bell for a few minutes.

But he will.

He sees me. Dark, dark hair, down past my shoulders. Giant glasses. Same blue baggies but with black hi-top all-stars crossed up with blue laces. Black Bad Company shirt, the one with the glitter reefer leaf. Dark blue bomber. Yup. He knows.

"Royal Killer!" he yells.

I laugh, look for a place to stash my books. The Greek in the sandwich place is putting the key in the door, getting ready for the good kids and the neighborhood old men to head over for coffee and baklava.

"Hey, George," I say. "Can I set my books in here for a second? I'll just stack 'em up on that phone book pile."

"Sure, sure, Theo," he says. "No problem." All the Greek people I know like to call me Theo instead of Teddy or Midget or whatever.

I step just inside the entryway and set my books down on top of his Yellow Pages archives, lean right back out onto the sidewalk.

Jethro, or whatever the hell this clown's name is, is about thirty yards off. I don't want to fuck up Georgie's place so I yell, "C'mon punk ass! Let's take it to the grass! GLK!" and start walking across Addison to the giant lawn in front of this school that's a square city block.

He closes the gap quick, so now I'm jogging backward talking shit.

"Ima beat your ass, punk!" I let him know, trying to be thoughtful.

"Fuck you Injun! Royal Killer!" his vocabulary kinda lacking.

"Let's do it, motherfucker!" I say, encouragingly.

"RK all day!" he yells.

Jeezus this is weak, I think.

"Alright ya hillbilly cousin fucker!" I say. "Come get some!"

Probably shouldn'ta said that, I think, since my great-great-grand-parents from Tennessee were first cousins. Shit. Anyway,

"Let's humbug!"

He comes at me having seen too many Bruce Li movies and not enough Bruce Lee ones. He's got his hands moving in front of him, but they're just for show, not doing anything. I have to decide do I want to punch through that shit, or am I going to try and aikido this asshole.

As I punch this Gaylord in the face, I think,

Out in the field, all these whites.

He closes on me then. Grabs me under the armpits, trying to throw me to the ground. Hmmm.

Muskrat didn't understand the horde of white people out in what used to be a swamp, somewhere between Algonquin and Ottawa. Illinois this way was flat, and white, and windy, mostly. He watched a man in a hat, could smell his sweat meeting polyester, the man-made

fibers releasing noxious gases and a particular heat signature that were all unsettling. Muskrat was full, had eaten a bunch of dropped potato salad that was giving him indigestion, and so he decided to observe these humans. He saw quite a bit, witnessing what he supposed were their courtship rituals, and speculated they might be in big trouble.

I knee him in the balls. He screams, but not too loud. I look at him lying on the ground and

He also decided that he understood even less why they were lighting floating lanterns and sending them across this dried-out field, but there they were. These humans. Just. Not. Smart.

I grab up a handful of his dirty blonde hair (the grease, jeezus) and yank him around

Jenny wasn't sure who this guy was, or why she kept listening to his drivel, other than she thought it might be good to get laid at her sister's wedding. It was warm, she was drunk, and it really was a beautiful evening. She didn't care that his favorite band was Rush, but that should've told her some things. She liked R.E.O. Speedwagon, figured both bands started with "R," so good enough. They drank some more, managed to keep from throwing up (both complained about the potato salad and had that to keep coming back to when the conversation thinned), and generally thought sex with each other wouldn't be horrible. She was on the pill, and he was fixed; there was that.

So his face is looking at mine upside down. I pick up my foot and, royal-blue laces flashing,

As he rooted around on top of her, barely keeping it up, but yeah okay, that's pretty good right there, she thought, the lanterns started to come down. White blips and lights turned to fire on the extinct arid prairie and raced her way. She turned her face from the heat and thought, hurry up already.

I stomp on the crest of his nose, the bridge and the left orbital making that one sound and

Muskrat just stared back.

14. FOREVER YOUNG

But so far as the portage at Chicago was concerned this change
of sovereignty made little difference. What with the constant strife
among the savage tribes whose normal condition was that of warfare,
and the dangers to the whites caused by the neglect of military protec-
tion, the region was left a solitude; and the few references to its existence during a hundred years indicate confused relations between the
tribes and the few whites who ventured to visit the region.

—J. SEYMOUR CURREY, *THE STORY OF OLD FORT DEARBORN*, 1912

This gangbanger thing never leaves you, never goes away.
Even if you want it to.

Much later in life, I'll find myself at an academic conference, this one in Minneapolis of all places. I've never been here
before, but it's a pretty big city, makes me comfortable.

I'm alone, the way I usually like it. I need to eat something, and
after being on the unfriendly and miserly East Coast for ten years
or so, I'm excited to be back in the Midwest where people say hi
back and serve you normal portions of food. I know my team is in
town so the game will be on and I'm looking forward to watching

it, a luxury never provided out East, unless we make the playoffs or play the jesuswhofuckingcaresalreadyBostonRedSox. I find a bar near the dorms where I'm staying.

I tell the bartender I'm here to watch this White Sox game, currently in progress.

And I say,

"Don't get mad at me, but we are going to beat your ass."

He wipes out a glass with a bar towel, considers me and my statement, laughs.

"We'll see," he says.

Jermaine Dye hits a grand slam about five minutes later. I can even tell you the date and the inning—May 21, 2009, in the fourth—because all I have to do is Google "Jermaine Dye's grand slam beats Minnesota's ass."

I order up some wings (a shit ton in a small order) and some potato skins (even more).

I have a pop with my food because I never have understood the food and liquor thing. I just don't get it. Beer and pizza. Margaritas and nachos. These should be mutually exclusive things.

After I eat, I start drinking. Like the business it is.

I look over from the TV to the mirror behind the bar as people walk in and out. Old habits die hard.

A buddy-to-be of mine shows up. He's at least one of my tribes— nerd. Even has glasses and fucked-up teeth, just like me. We've never met before, but we recognize each other right away. Turns out he's a mixed-blood Crow. I'm an *iyeska* Lakota/Anishinaabe/ Mohawk who is obviously here for the conference, this being a weird sports bar near the hotel for our meeting. I, covered in tattoos, having hair to my ass and a Black Panther–style leather jacket hanging on the back of my stool with books stuffed in the pockets, am not the typical clientele. We ain't cousins, but we're *cousins.*

About four or five beers in, the White Sox with a comfortable lead on their way to the win I promised the bartender, these two guys walk in. One is about my age, the other one is older, like an uncle. They're Native, too. The guy my age is wearing a red hoodie. Looks just like my old bro GoofGoof, a fellow Simon City Royal and a Choctaw with a fucked-up Indian nose and ill-repaired hare-lip, but he seems familiar from somewhere else, besides. My brain whirls through its Rolodex. I don't know too many folks in academia yet, and besides, these cats dress like me, not like these professor-type nerds. I needa talk to this guy.

Easy enough, he walks right up to me, uncle in tow.

"What's up, Peoples," he says, eyeing the big-ass bent right-eared Playboy bunny tattoo with a blue diamond eye and a gold tooth tattooed on my arm.

"You see it, Folks," I give back.

"Hunh," he says.

"Hunh," I say. "Have a seat, bruh," I continue.

Him and the uncle pull up a couple of stools into the aisle and sit down across from me and the Crow.

"Where you from?" I ask. This right here is how folks introduce themselves to each other: tell your tribe, your family, your relations. But he knows this ain't what I wanna know. He eyes me up and down, that same glimmer of rec I'm feeling too flickers in his eyes.

"Kilbourn Park," he says. "How 'bout you?"

"Touhy and Ridge. Farwell and Clark," I say.

It's on now.

"Yeah. I thought you looked . . . familiar," he says. "You're a Royal, hunh?"

"Yeah, Folks," I say. "You're a Gaylord, hunh?" I say, Kilbourn Park being a main branch of that set. "And 'shnaab?" I say.

"Yup. What are you? A Sioux or something?"

"Yup. Alright, den," I say.

And we look at each other for a while. A good long while.

His uncle picks up the vibe. "What are you two doing?" the uncle says.

"Nothing," we both reply.

The Crow sips his beer, eyes ping-ponging back and forth on us.

Me and this Ojibway GL watch each other, meaning we watch each other's eyes. That's where violence happens, hints at its own oncoming escalation and arrival. It's in the lids, the subtle raisings, widenings. As you talk, talk shit, maybe even talk through things, you watch the eyes—it's where acceptance, rejection, calculation all happen. You can watch the consideration of the moves they want to make and then see them coming if they're on the way.

Quiet edges of light crawl over and into the folds on his oversized sweatshirt with its hood bunched up across his shoulders. The soft rays come in different colors from the TV and the neon beer signs, but they're mostly pale blue. They make me think of spirits, and that starts to fill the space between us. Back in Chicago we're deadly opposition, but here in Minnesota, both of us with Anishinaabe ancestors, well, yeah. I want to think about what's happening here. The Crow senses it, raises an eyebrow above his crooked glasses.

"Wait," he says. "What's going on with you two?"

"Nothing," we reply.

He takes a sip of his beer, laughs a little.

"I don't believe that for a minute," he says.

"For real, homes," I say. "What are you talking about?"

"Well," he says, "You guys are—"

"Are what?" the GL asks.

"Yeah, what?" I add.

"Do you guys know each other?" he says.

"Yeah, we do," I say. "Kinda."

"But not in a good way," the Crow says.

"Yeah," says the GL.

"So are you guys . . . enemies, or something?" the Crow asks.

"Nah," we say. "Well, yeah," we each go, almost in sync.

"So are you two gonna fight or something?"

I look at him, the anticipation on his face, its voyeuristic flavor starting to piss me off.

"I don't think so," I say.

The Gaylord looks me up and down.

I give him the one-eyebrow raise.

"Nah," he says, to both of us.

"But you would. You could?" the Crow throws in.

"We could," I say, looking at the GL, returning the up-and-down.

"We could," he echoes back, tryna stare me down, now.

"But we probably won't," I say, staring back.

The Crow offers, "But if we were in Chicago—"

"But we ain't," I cut him off, all these buts making me uncomfortable.

The uncle jumps in. "Knock it off, alla ya's."

"No problem," his nephew says.

"Yeah, no problem," I say. "We're cool." The guitar riff from "I Heard the Owl Call My Name" plays in my head, and I try to imagine explaining a humbug with some out-of-town GL to my department head out on the East Coast from the pay phone in a Minneapolis jail. "We're cool," I repeat.

But we're not. The more we drink, the more we talk about our old neighborhoods and tell old stories, the tenser it gets.

I bring up Spy. I can't help it.

"You guys should be ashamed of yourselves. That wasn't right," the GL says. "A sword? What the fuck is wrong with you?"

"Hey. Necessity is the mother of invention."

He looks me up and down, squints, pretty drunk right about now.

"That don't make it right, Royal," he says.

"It is what it is, Folks," I say, pretty drunk my damn self.

It's what boys do and men shouldn't do, this cockfight drama born of pressure and impulse. We grow out of it as long as the night is dry, but if you're a gangbanger, well, that presents a different set of rules that apply themselves at usually inopportune moments, even if you're two cities from home. And if you're in a city anywhere, you're never far enough from home.

As I sit here wondering what necessity might need me to invent and I feel that ability slip out of my increasingly drunk grasp, my Crow buddy slides into my field of vision, teeth at the lead.

"What now?" he whispers.

"Hunh?" I manage back.

"Are you guys going to fight, or what?" he continues with the low talk. I think, man, this guy needs to clean his glasses.

"Dude. I think that's his auntie there too, having a beer. What's wrong with you?" I say.

"I don't know. Well, you know—"

"Yeah. You don't know. So you should drop it." His shit is really starting to bug me.

"I just think it's crazy you guys would fight about . . . whatever it is you would fight about," he says.

"Me too," I say, "but that's how it is."

He wants to know *more*. He's a scholar after all, and that's how it works. My mind races, preps up a five-minute minimum diatribe on turf and blood feud and revenge and how gangbanging replaces a lost sense of family, how it provides coming-of-age ceremony, particularly for those whose tribal customs have been largely erased through urban relocation, how it's a form of *hunka*, of relative making, of belonging and neo-tribalization, but I don't.

Because I'm so

tired.

And I want to say that it's because he looks like Goof, who's rotting away in a prison somewhere, life wasted, or that I have some kind of blood memory of the Anishinaabe relocation program forced on my Lakota ancestors in some kind of twisted way that forgets my own Ojibwe ancestry, or that I'm losing myself somehow to another government program designed to assimilate us, this time into academia, a state apparatus, my colonized self out here professing to know a thing or two in the world.

But I'm not.

"Let me by you a drink, Peoples," I say.
    I'm saying goodbye to my youth.
    "Sure, Folks," he says.
    Just not forever.

15. COYOTE DRINKS

We drink long and deep in the heart of Blackfeet territory. Well maybe, maybe not their territory, but still territory they liked to claim they at least walked through. On their way to do some dark shit to a tribe we just won't name. But they know who it is.

It's me and the Poet Laureate of Baa'oogeedí. I'm not the anything of anywhere, just the chronicler of this shit right here. But if I had to be something, it might be the Scribus Bacchus of any place around the corner in your neighborhood.

We don't have any of our Blackfeet guides with us, and we're on our own out here in some shitbird town west of the world. Fuck. We don't even have our Kootenai guide with us, the one who would get puffy when his white friends were around. It's dark and still warm outside. We find our way to the Gold Doubloon, or the Wooden Nickel, or the something or other. It's been a good night. A good night to get out of the bougie bar where we had been getting those stares earlier. Usually it's not a big deal. But some nights, well, fuck that.

The poet grabs a couple of seats in the back, by the jukebox. We talk about how we're gonna stuff that motherfucker, play six hours of Prince and just get fucked up. But we don't. Okay. Maybe five bucks worth only. But still. All Prince.

I decide we need some drinks, and quick. I head up to the bar. The scary bartender, the bullet in a T-shirt, hair skinned right off down to the eyebrows, he remembers me from some time before, says, Hey, what's up. Scary-faced tattoos wink at me under the too-close neon. I'm like cider, man, with a big glass of ice and a gin and tonic. You laugh, but cider is good, and one of my bros, he tells me the Irish say if you drink it, your feet won't stink. Well, yeah. Ain't nobody wants stinky feet.

The Bullet, he grabs up a pint glass from under the bar. It's a frosty bastard, and I'm thinking alright. This'll be a good drink. But it ain't for me. Shit. He fills it full of ice and almost to the top with gin. Waves the tonic gun at it. Hahahaha, fuck. Gonna be some poetic blackout tonight. I get my kinda dumpy definitely unfuckingmajestic glass of ice, no frost, but maybe a ash or a fruit fly in there, fill it up, chug what's left in the bottle, and leave the empty on the bar, low and slow fiction writer headed back to our table, weak enough to be a designated driver for someone who gives slightly less of a shit than I do.

Me and the poet, we talk. 'Bout all kinds of shit. This good night had been a good day, had been that one day in the fall when the leaves change just right and you look down the long street and that light looks like it's coming from below instead of above, the golds and the reds rising up from the road and floating up into the dark green of the trees, the canopy close but the light pushing you up with it as far as you can imagine, and you don't feel hemmed in, you don't feel like someone else's weight is on your neck, and you can see and feel and breathe all at the same time, and that light that washes over your eyes and into your heart, the light that flicks along the edges of your soul and fills all the tears and the gouges?

That's the light you don't get to see too often so you fucking say hello to it the day it shows up.

We're saying our hellos to those kinds of days and talking about nights we missed, nights we'd never know here, but nights we knew from certain places in Arizona and South Dakota. We're maudlin in our love for those places and thirsty for those stories, and we drink and drink, and that certain light, that one kind of light is with us, light that could be seen in other spaces and by other faces. We know that as we lift those words and stories into the air and we can see them hanging there. Then the moment comes when we know we can't take them back, their lights ringing in the loud but lonely space around the table where we sit.

He sees us before we see him. We knew but didn't know he would come, dared a conjure we thought we couldn't, knew we shouldn't, but like reckless teenagers we do it anyway, a double-dog dare.

And now he's here.

"Wait. Hey, man. You guys are . . . skins!"

Shit.

Guess who.

"What?" we struggle to come back from the world we just wove, the world that held us warm and safe, the strands dissipating in the harshness of his breath, his words.

"Nah, man. Well, yeah, what? We're just hanging out."

"Here, hold my cue."

What the fuck.

I knew better. The poet, maybe not.

See, that right there? The "hold my cue?" The poet took that cue, and all the others that would follow, and dang. You know what that means. Sonofabitch.

"Wanna play pool?"

He doesn't really want *us* to play, morelike wants us to watch him play. We kind of oblige him, but really we're trying to shake off that dust he just laid on us. I manage pretty good, but the poet and his pints of gin and tonics, well, he's pure fucked. He looks over to him and says, "You have a beautiful face."

Ah, shit.

So the him. Maybe forty, maybe sixty years old. Of course, you couldn't tell. Medium color skin. Hair he might've cut himself. Or maybe Iktomi did it for him after they wrestled for the scissors and he lost. Most, but not all, of his teeth. I look him deep in that beautiful face, and all the teeth he was missing were the same ones I was missing. Big brown eyes. Eyes that never really leave your face. Parts of a mustache. Six, maybe seven chin hairs. A T-shirt older than either of my kids, and my youngest is in high school. Draggy jeans, the color of salt in the desert. The bottoms of his pants just sort of end, fade into the floor. Not an ounce of fat on him. He grabs his cue back from the poet and then stalks the pool table like a twist of coat hanger wrapped around a stick. He drinks his beer one glass at a time. It'll be full, he'll drain it all at once, and then it will be full again, right after he sets it down. He never leaves the pool table, but I register zero surprise every time I watch him empty a glass down his ever-jumping, seemingly endless throat. I kinda wish we had our Blackfeet guides around as I watch him devour beer after beer. His drinking is so clean, so fierce it inspires the shit out of me. I knock back about four ciders in an hour, and I'm like damn. He is of course about five ahead of me, but no shame. You do what you can when you drink with him. Prince urges me to go crazy in what I feel are real sincere ways, and you know you gotta listen to Prince, regardless. The poet must've been looking at him too, because I hear him say,

"You have a beautiful face."

Shit. The poet was a goner. I'm on my own for this one.

I drop my drinking into low gear. Not like "can I have an ice water" or some bullshit like that, but I throttle it back.

He beats the ass off all the whites at the pool tables, runs game on two or three at the same time. Now they owe him money, so they slink away just like all their ancestors, suddenly uncomfortable with the whole back part of this bar and acting like he doesn't exist. He looks around, surveys the billiardian destruction he's wrought. Smiles to himself. Smiles deeper to himself, satisfaction in a shoving match with confidence for smile of the month.

"So hey." He slaps his hand on our table. "I'm Lakota and Diné. How about you guys? Where you guys from?"

"Uh (something in Diné)."

"Where?"

"White Cone. It's in Arizo—"

"Oh. You're Navajo?"

"Yeah. Holy shit . . . You know, you have a beautiful face."

"What about you?"

"I'm Sihasapa. Born and raised in Chicago."

"Yeah? Yeah. That's cool. We're gonna party."

Fuck.

"Yup. Diné and Lakota. We. Are. Gonna. *Party*."

The poet, he's about this shit. I feel the claws sinking in, trying to grab me around the wrist. I pull back. I say,

"I need to take a piss."

I head to the bathroom. It's like taking a leak in a trough behind the half-pushed-in folding door of a cheap closet, with a clinkety fan next to your head, while you hope no one busts in and hits you in the face with the broken brass barrel lock that hasn't been painted in twenty years, the one you're staring at while you try to hurry and breathe through your nose.

I zip up, walk out, remember I finished my drink before I went in (because, yeah, that's what you do in certain places, with certain people), and get ready to head up to the bar for another one. I stop back at the table, where the boys are partying like it's 1999.

"Anyone need a drink?" This is really directed at the poet, since magic pants over there, well, his glass is full, of course.

"Oh, yeah. That'd be guhreat," he laughs, that famous laugh of his.

Hahahaha. He's fucking hammered.

Oh shit. He's fucking hammered.

Sometimes you drink too much, and St. Christopher takes care of you. I think he got in trouble, though, for hanging out with drunks, isn't much of a saint anymore. My dad, world-class drunk, always had a St. Christopher medal. And it got him out of most of the shit. For instance, he only went to jail once after he turned sixty. That medallion had some big medicine in it. Shiiiiiit. It was the one thing my uncle asked for when the old man passed. But tonight? The old man's medallion and a couple more weren't about to help us here. Fuck.

"Two more, sir."

Bullet, he looks up at me. But just to the side of me. Like he can see what's looming, who waits. Like there's someone standing there. I shift my eyes in the mirror behind the bar. Nope. There's no one there.

"Coming right up," he laughs a little.

I shudder just a bit. Look around. There're a few hipsters drinking PBRs that've been kept warm on purpose. Good for you, assholes, I say, but not too loud. I imagine people don't like to be called assholes, even if they are. There are beards, and new flannels, and what we called birth-control specs when they were issued to us in boot camp. The guffaws are forced and annoying, but Bullet gives no fucks, gets the drinks. This place has peanuts on the tables and shells on the floors. I look at a paper rectangle of peanuts and then over at the spit-flecked beard of some asshole with a rectangle tattooed on his hand, and I pass on the possibility of being infected with some kind of fatal whiteness, a malaise for which there may never be a cure. I shake my head ever so slightly as I head back to our table.

He waits.

"You drinking or what!?"

"Yeah, man. I'm drinking," I say. "So is he."

"Well drink up. What are you waiting for?!"

"Nothing, man. We're drinking."

"So where do you work?"

Fuck. I really don't want to do this.

"You have a really beautiful face," the poet's eyes wander above the rim of his glass.

Sonofabitch.

"So. Huh? Where do you work?"

"In town, man," I say. "How about you?"

"I do construction. Let's go."

"Where to? Where we going?" I don't know this town much at all.

"You have a beautiful face. It's like . . ."

"My place. We're gonna party."

I look down. At my glass. Take a big drink. Then over at those not-quite-white jeans. And where they end. I don't think he's wearing any shoes.

"Well hold on. We got some time. Let's finish these."

"It's like classic, classical. Like in a Curtis photo. It's really beautiful."

"Well hurry up, man." His fingers are annoyed, roll triplets on the table.

Shit. We're done for. The way he's looking at me? Fuck.

You know those moments, those ones that require deep commitment, when you know something is going to happen you don't want to happen, but there's no way out of the situation, so you commit to being in that situation, but you commit to making it right, no matter what?

Yeah. This was definitely one of those moments.

Son. Of. A. Bitch.

The poet, he's drinking, laughing that famous laugh. Doing his thing. But our new friend? Every time I look up, yeah. He's looking right at me. Even when he's waltzing around the pool tables, he's looking me in the face. I catch him once when he's making a round, and I look down quicklike, and still can't tell if he has shoes on. What the fuck. I mean he must have shoes, right? It's a fucking bar. This is a weird town, but who doesn't wear shoes to a bar? I laugh to myself. They're old-ass sandals or something, whatever.

England Dan and John Ford Coley are describing what waits for us. I chug my drink. The poet just straight fucking downs his like it's an ice water, and I have to sniff the glass when he's done and ain't looking, cause, holy shit. Nope. Juniper. Man.

Our older brother? He's dumping his beer down that deep throat of his, looking over his glass at me, not blinking, just drinking, and then, bam, the beer is gone and he sets his glass down, hard, still looking at me.

"You know you have a beautiful face . . ."

We both look at the poet.

We laugh.

"Let's go."

I get up, dragging ass a bit, but we head out the front door, generous and friendly "later bros" to the Bullet.

We walk down the street. It's a pretty nice night, the just-right bookend to the beautiful day. I think, man, we need to get something to eat. There's just . . . too much going on here. Need to slow it down. Deaden the course of the alcohol uptaking from the veins.

"Let's go to the Oxford."

"The what?" he says, herding the poet north.

I say it again.

"What for?" he asks.

"Grab a little something to eat."

"Hmmm. Okay, I guess. Let's go." He cuts back a little, pairs the poet off to me, lopes ahead some. He moves fast. Like you think he would. But not so fast that we can't follow. Ditto. Me and the poet, we move okay. I look, and the poet, he's drinking a can of beer, a tall boy. Where the fuck did that come from?

I must've made a sound, since our boy laughs, sharp and loud, because, ha! I think, it's a can of PBR. This, he seems to find funny. But he laughs to himself, and at us, not with us. He looks over his own beer at us, name on the can unheard of, walking backward, pace unchanging, eyes unblinking. He throws the empty can over his shoulder and turns back to the street. Me and the poet slosh along, almost catching up.

"Did you see his face? It's beautiful."

"Hey man. We're going to get something to eat."

"Where?"

"The Oxford."

"Really?"

"Yup."

"And then are we going over to his place?"

"Yeah, sure," I say, thinking, mind racing, how the fuck are we going to get out of this? "Whatever you want to do. But let's go eat first."

"Where at?"

"The Oxford."

"Oh yeah."

The Oxford. The Oxford is a bar/restaurant type place, well yeah, officially it's a saloon. It has slot machines, brains and eggs, shitty beer; Budweiser is the imported stuff. Not that there's anything wrong with that (ha!), but yeah. It's that kind of place. And the food is pretty good. The whole thing is open twenty-four hours, has been for years, I don't even think they have keys anymore, but they shut the liquor down at some point in the evening, and people sort of drift over into the booths and tables away from the bar. Other people come in from other bars, other places, fresh off of whatever they've been doing elsewhere. Some of them look like whatever they've been doing is downright unsavory, but hey, that's their business. We're going there to eat, not to judge.

We get to the Oxford before the crush, before the too-loud talking and too-earnest laughing that mark the inebriated begin to show. Me and the poet take a seat along the wall near the door. We've been here before. Our boy has disappeared for the moment—I hope it turns into an even longer run—and pick up a menu.

The poet laureate is kinda laughing to himself, reading the menu and doubtless wondering at the conjecture of food and words and the jargony, old-timey names for some of the plates: "He Needs 'Em" (Brains & Eggs), "Overland Trout" (Roast Pork), "Slow Elk" (Roast Beef), and "Inside Job" (Liver), etc. I look over the menu halfheartedly, kind of because I know what I want, and kind of because the vibe is weird. I'm keeping my eyes open.

Our boy drifts back to our table. He's been over at the bar just as it's closing. He shows us his prizes: two clear plastic bottles of, I don't know, corn likker? Maybe it's vodka. I shudder a little. He seems *super* excited. The poet looks at the bottles, holds them up to the light. His one eye blobs out, blows up real big through the plastic when I look over at him as brings the bottles slowly back down to the table. He reminds me of a goldfish my friend won at the St. Hilary's carnival in the abandoned IHOP parking lot back in Chicago, the one where I won two cartons of smokes. I think I won four actually on their wheel of fortune, but because I was like twelve, they only gave me half my winnings. Fucking Catholics.

"We're gonna party."

Shit, man. I just want to eat, and say,

"Hold on, man. We need to eat."

"Maybe you do, but we need to get drinking." He looks over at the poet, who's humming to himself.

I'm about to make some probably unwise smartass comment when the waiter shows up.

"Out."

"Whu?"

"Out. Out! OUT!"

"Dude. What is wrong with you?"

The waiter, who looks like a cross between Leslie Jordan and Michael Jeter, and reminds me of a hostile Les Nessman, is starting to yell louder at us. Now, granted, he's stiffed us before, made us wait like forty-five minutes before we up and left, treated us like shit before, and generally acted like the racist asshole that he is, but this was new.

"Man. What is your problem?" I ask.

"Just get out."

"Nah. What? Why?"

"H-h-h-h, w-w-wh."

"What?" I say.

"Just get out!"

He calls over some ploppy security dude in a nylon gold windbreaker. I'm all,

"Hey. Calm down. I just want to know why he won't wait on us."

"I don't know, but you need to go." Little Yellowjacket rent-a-cop starts to get in my face.

"Fuck. C'mon. Let's go," I say.

Jordan/Jeter/Nessman is apoplectic.

I hope he has a geyser or something. I really fucking hate this guy.

Our boy looks at him. Doesn't say a word. Just gets up. And leaves. All the way to the door, he never takes his eyes off the sputtering waiter, whose face is turning pink, red, redder. The silver temples on his glasses start to sink into the sides of his reddening head. His eyes dart around, the far-sighted lenses magnifying whatever the fuck is driving his tiny madness.

I smile at him big. All the way back to where the gaps from my missing teeth show. The poet, he keeps chuckling. The waiter drops his pad, and by the time he gets it picked up, we're gone, twists of smoke where our bodies were standing. The little bell rings as the door closes shut.

Down the street we go. Weave, bob, drink. We trudge for miles. All the while he lopes along up front doing that just-out-of-reach thing you struggle to keep up with so that you're not really thinking about what you're doing.

Until the poet stops to take a leak.

We come to an abrupt halt by a discount tire place, the poet pissing in the sagebrush out back. The fluorescent light gives everyone's face that real unpleasant cast, the one where everybody looks like they didn't make the cut for the *Less Than Zero* club scene but the on-set lighting stayed with them anyway. We hear the zipper come up, and I gain my senses for a minute.

"You know, I really need to get him home," I say.

"Nah."

"No. I do. It's been a long day. He's been up since like five this morning."

"So?"

"So that's a long day. He needs to get some sleep."

"That's not a long day at all. Not for me it's not."

"Well, he's not you, so . . ."

"So let's get moving."

Damn it.

The poet, he just laughs that laugh.

Back in the street, walking. I've never seen a place like this before, wouldn't even think this neighborhood would be considered part of the city. The street winds around, gets a little wilder, less populated. The light is a constant yellow, buzzing out of old arc lamps. The poet laughs and drinks. We're shitfaced and humming shy of the streetlights, glancing down and wincing away, but I manage to send for an uber, thinking we're close . . . r.

We *walk*. So fucking typical, when you're suddenly magically young and ripped—we throw drinks up in the air, hide from the cops, piss in the street, laugh too loud, and shush each other when porch lights come on. The air stays warm, gets damp. We can hear cars on a highway, whooshing low and intermittent, like an alarm you can just barely hear, so you sleep on through it.

Then:

"Just around the corner. Go down that way," and we're at his place.

He lives in an alley for fuck's sake. It's small trailer, jammed in a parking space behind a building, lined right up, nuts-to-butts with three or four abandoned trailers. Well, maybe not abandoned, but uninhabited and sad, if that helps. Harsh fluorescent light angles down from a utility pole over the scene, makes big shadows out of the places it doesn't reach. Him and the poet head inside.

I take a piss next to a wiry sumac and then look in his trailer. He's standing next to a table where the poet is seated, drinking from the plastic bottle in one hand and out of a warm can in the other, blue slatted shadowed light defining both their shapes. My eyes trace their faces, and I look left then, away from the poet. My gaze comes to rest on those almost-white jeans, the ones the color of desert salt, the ones that fade away into dregs, torn edges that just hide what I knew would be there, a pair of wide, brown paws. When I look up at his face, it's looking back at me, and the arms it belongs to are bracing themselves, one hand on the edge of the table, the other on the counter. I back out of the trailer slowly, my eyes never leaving his, and say,

"Looks like the car's here. See? Here it is, on my phone. C'mon," I say. "Let's go then."

He lunges at me from the trailer, his teeth snap over the shoulder of the poet, inches from my face, but we back out, me holding the poet's hand.

"You have a beautiful face," that one says.

"Good night, Old One," I say.

Good night.

The Potawatomi traded for this?

    "It does appear cruel, Grandfather."

    It is, in fact. Are they at least going to eat these animals?

"No. They're for looking at."

So, they'll spend their live locked in these cages? That seems particularly cruel, grandson.

    "It does."

We were making our way through Lincoln Park Zoo, that great, free showcase of Western opulence and magnanimity in the heart of Chicago's North Side. The neighborhood used to be interesting and diverse, but now it's the home of million-dollar-plus mansions, more akin to John Hughes's cinematic Winnetka than anything remotely urban, chock full of apple-cheeked cops, overpriced restaurants, and franchise shit shows that parade eight-hundred-dollar scarves and cups of coffee for slightly less.

Where are these animals from?

"All over the world."

Are they captured there? Born here?

"It's a mix. They have breeding programs for many of them."

It's more cruel than I had thought, then.

"Yup. It is."

I knew his Sauk name was Ma-ka-tai-me-she-kia-kiak, meant "be a black hawk,"

thought,

I probably shouldn't take him to the raptor exhibit on the off chance—

Grandson, we need to do something.

Though he's barely visible, and his voice is just above a whisper, I jump and say,

"Like what?"

His eyes gleam across countless planes.

I'll show you. Come with me.

We walk for a bit and then we're in the Lion House. We stroll past a few cages, stop at the first one with a visible occupant.

His spectral hand reaches out, coalesces in this world, grabs the iron grate. His now-solid fingers deftly open the door to the cheetah cage. A young female registers his presence with a baring of her fangs, a feline smile and squinting of her eyes acknowledging his gesture as she walks out of the cage, steps down into the cement space between the ledge and the black metal slats, and effortlessly jumps over the handrail. She silently pads toward the glinting sunlight of the open door, the boisterous zoo patrons stunned into silence.

That's a beautiful being right there, grandson.

I agree, watching her hips sway, exit the building.

We make our way down the row, stop to marvel at the jaguar.

He repeats the motions, and the ruler of the Mayan Underworld springs into the passageway, heads for the open double doors.

This seems the right thing to do, grandson.

"I agree, Grandfather."

Civets, servals, lynx, and ocelots freed, we continue through the zoo, releasing all of their relatives. Buffalo, wolves, giraffes, and elk low their way into the lakefront woods.

Do they imprison winged ones in this place as well?

"They do."

Show me.

We head to the Bird House.

He shakes his head.

This is inexcusable.

"It is."

He smiles over my shoulder, watches a polar bear with a chicken in its mouth rumble past the closing glass doors.

He reaches up with both arms, closes his eyes.

The glass walls and ceiling

dissolve,

the standing iron frames breathe lonely and out of place, disappear.

Hundreds of bird eyes roll up to an indescribable horizon, pour through now-open space, take flight in a riot of flapping wings.

He smiles.

Look at this, grandson.

17. INDIAN WARS

We passed Chicago and observed that the fort had been evacuated by the Americans, and their soldiers had gone to Fort Wayne. They were attacked a short distance from the fort and defeated. They had a considerable quantity of powder in the fort at Chicago, which they had promised to the Indians, but the night before they marched away, they destroyed it by throwing it into a well. If they had fulfilled their word to the Indians, they doubtless would have gone to Fort Wayne without molestation.

—MA-KA-TAI-ME-SHE-KIA-KIAK (BLACK HAWK)

JD shot me in the chest with a pellet gun. And not one of those Daisy pumps either. This was the .45 looking one with the CO2 canisters.

"You motherfucker! Goddamn, that hurts!"

"Hahaha, Teddy! Fuck you." He wheeled backward, me holding my heart with my left hand and taking a swing at that smirky face of his with my right.

Son of a bitch. It really did hurt. I stuck my hand inside my big, loose royal-blue and black flannel, pulled it back out, blood smeared on my fingers. I went back in and fished out the lead pellet, tapped my finger on the still-pointy end, and flicked it over my shoulder. I'm pissed now, Bruce Lee style. Not because of the puckered scar it'll leave (cool points, of course), but because now I had a hole in my favorite shirt. This shirt cost me twenty minutes of skilled dancing with the undercover security dick while I stole it from Zayre's. Damnit. I worked for this one.

We were playing, I don't know, Army? Nope. It was Cowboys and Injuns. That's right. That's why I had this shitty pump rifle and the Jimmys1&3 and JD had those nice automatics. That made perfect sense.

Yup. Those assholes were bored and Jimmy1 had all these BB and pellet guns just like his old man who filled his own shells had all these real guns. Jimmy1 said "let's play Army" and that turned into "Cavalry" real quick after he handed out the guns and everyone realized what they had.

I played along, but I knew in the back of my mind what was going to happen. I thought about what I was going to have to do and counted myself lucky I was wearing these big old glasses, cause if these guys were even remotely thinking like I was, someone was gonna lose an eye.

Jimmy1 lived in this big red-brick three-story courtyard building on Damen Avenue right off Fargo where his dad was the janitor. I think in New York they call them supers or something; but here in fuckin' RealTown Chicago you're a goddamn janitor. Big Louie had this building and one other small one down the street that was on the way to the bar, so it all worked out real well for him. I always thought it was cool that Jimmy1 got to live with both his parents. His ma became my ma when she adopted me in that way that mas do. She was a waitress around the corner from where his pop drank. Shit, now that I think about it, all of our mas were waitresses, except for JD's. She was a traitor-ass Latin Queen, so who knows and who cares what the fuck she did.

It was summer, but it was daytime, so we basically had the run of this giant building all to ourselves because everyone was at work, except for the drunks and the addicts, and those assholes never leave their apartments, so no worries. We grabbed our weapons and headed out the apartment down to the lobby and onto the grass in front. Decided it was every man for himself, and since I had been pumping this piece of shit since I got it fifteen minutes ago I turned and shot Jimmy1 in the neck. Just missed that eye.

"Ow! Fuck you!" He popped off a shot that hit me in leg.

It didn't hurt, so I laughed and started running south across the face of the building, pumping the living shit out of this piece of crap, getting set for when I'd let him catch up with me. At least you could pack the rifle full of BBs then just pull the slide back when you were ready. I didn't look to see if anyone was behind me, and I had no idea where anyone else went.

I headed for the long gangway that ran under the building on the right-hand side as you faced it, the one that went almost all the way back to the alley. Off the path of its walk were the rear stairwells to the back doors of each of the apartments. On Friday afternoons we'd go up and down all the porches and steal people's bottles to turn in for cash to go to the movies and buy booze. Every surface of the wooden stairs, railings, floors, and ceilings was painted that sexy-ass Chicago grey enamel.

The gangway smelled funky all year long, but of course even more in the summer heat, and today the humidity was crackin'. It reeked. I was dying out here. Sure, I wore a flannel but anyway with no T-shirt because if we needed to do some shoplifting, well, yeah. It was big and loose and Open Pantry had these bottles of flavored wine that would get you fuuuucked up. Quick stick a pair of those in the waist of your baggies with that big shirt hanging down and buy a Slim Jim and ask the cute girl behind the counter for a book of matches and it costs you twenty-nine cents to get wasted.

I made it almost to the end when JD popped out from the bottom of the stairs. Jimmy1 must've used his old man's spare keys to let him cut through one of the endless hallways that internally connect this beast of a building.

Bam! He laughed and I took that shot I was talking about at the beginning.

Like I said, I lunged at JD, took a swing, but the little weasel was too quick. I chased after him, getting ready to dig deep into my already expansive swear-word trough, the one recently enriched by a recent Cormac McCarthy read.

That's when I felt another shot, this one digging into my back. "Motherfucker!" I yelled, now loquacious in no ways, my trough icing over before my mind's eye. Jimmy1 had waited at the top of the stairs until I went tear-assing after JD.

I looked up through my watering eyes and saw that fucker JD, jogging backward, working the slide and getting ready to shoot me one more time and then run for good and then

Jimmy3 cracked JD in the back of the head with the butt of the other Daisy pump rifle. Now that I think about it, he might've got that piece of shit cause he was black, just sayin'.

Jimmy3 was about the only one from our set who wrote me when I was in the Navy. His letters were epic. They'd have clips about shootings and shit from our neighborhood and they'd be covered with bent-right-ear bunnies in top hats, 3-D crosses, and upside-down crowns galore. King Killer Queen Thriller VLK GLK UKK and six-points with cracked Vicky Lou stars below broken pyramids and horned hearts with pitchforks and dead klansmen abounding, and he'd ask me how I was doing Folks and tell me about all the stupid shit everyone was still doing. Glorious.

JD crumpled like a wet paper towel, and I ran up and kicked him in the nuts. I spit in his face and was about to put a knee in his throat when Jimmy1 grabbed my left arm from behind and tried to spin me around. I broke free and grabbed the barrel of my rifle, which wasn't shit for shooting anyway, and brought it down on the chain link fence that finished the line of the gangway out here near the alley. The stock snapped off and I held the barrel up under Jimmy1's chin as I pushed him back out of my space. His hands went up in the air.

"What's the matter, fucker?" I hissed out from closed teeth.

"Teddy, quit man," he said. "Peace."

"No shit, peace," I said. "There ain't never gonna be peace, motherfucker." Where did that come from? I thought.

"Man, calm down. It's me," he said.

"Yeah, yeah. Cool. Peace."

What the fuck am I doing?

These guys are my brothers, the only real family I got. Yeah, there's dysfunction like in any family, but dysfunction here will get you killed. You can't fuck around. We need each other. We're a pretty small set up here, and there's Kings on all sides. And now these Vice Lords. Plus I got PR Stones, Eagles, and Unknowns down where I live. Fuck. It happens this way, I think. Some of us have regular-way family, but they don't know this shit, care even less. "Don't get busted. I ain't coming to get you." "Don't get caught, dumbass." These are some of the loving instructions we get. So we have to raise ourselves, know and love each other, be there for everyone, no matter what. We police ourselves, feed ourselves, represent ourselves, and respect ourselves. It's a lot, but we're in charge, and I wouldn't have it any other way. Have I read *Lord of the Flies*? Yeah. Three or four times. I get it. I get that. But that's a book. This shit right here is for real. And if you fuck it up, you're gone. So there's constant negotiations between respect, and rights and responsibilities, and love. That's what it all boils down to. That warfare shit between sets? You're a Crown, you're a Hook, GD, Royal, whatever? Lots of times if you can talk, just *talk*, you can settle shit. Give respect, get respect. I got it worked out at school. Shit, it's all Kings and Vice Lords, but you know, you gamble a little, talk some shit at the right time, and well, you can get yourself a pass, that's all I'm saying. I go to school, do my shit, and we're good. So yeah, for now, that's the way it works.

That's why this Cowboys and Injuns shit is bogus. It was disrespectful and they knew it. Did it get a lil crazy? Well yeah. But this is

Cowboys and Injuns.

And

that shit ain't no joke.

18. GOLD COIN

Your own historians, true to their trust, have recorded the cruelty of their own race, that unborn millions might read it as a testimony against them. In the name of all that is sacred and dear to mankind, tell Pokagon, if you can, why less love, pity, or sympathy should be required of the civilized and enlightened people than of untutored savages.

—SIMON POKAGON, "THE MASSACRE OF FORT DEARBORN AT CHICAGO: GATHERED FROM THE TRADITIONS OF THE INDIAN TRIBES ENGAGED IN THE MASSACRE, AND FROM THE PUBLISHED ACCOUNTS"

Back in the day you could tell the people who never thought they'd live to see thirty.

I mean why the fuck else would you tattoo your hands? Do you ever think about when you thought about living to see thirty? How far off that would be? How you might get hit by the proverbial bus, or by a five iron like the one Latin King that Frankie took out on Clark Street? Did the thought "at least I won't have to live to thirty" maybe pass through that Playboy Bunny's head as it caromed off the side of Belmont Towers by Lake Michigan on the way down to the sidewalk when she jumped from the roof after Hef and Co. fired her? How about, "Thirty? Shiiiit, I can't believe I'm stuck at seventy" passing through the mind of that old lady by the John Hancock building a few winters ago right as an eight-by-twelve-foot sheet of ice that had silently peeled away from the eighty-third floor sliced her in half and left her Pomeranian wondering whether to shit or stay? Have you ever walked over a river on a bridge and thought about jumping, maybe Beelzebub or Astaroth whispering over your shoulder, or your own vertigoed brain daring your billowing soul? Will you now, the next time you cross one? Like the line that comes after "riding alone in the dark," when Marty is singing about El Paso and you're at the end of the bar with the old man, pretty drunk at sixteen, trying to keep up and thinking about heading out to see your boys before you puke; up in here, that's the one that plays in your head more than it should some days. There's just too many ways out there, too deep a rabbit hole to even risk spending more than a split second on it. I remember the first time I really listened to BOC's "Don't Fear the Reaper" and that shit made sense. It's really a wonder that more folks don't check out daily.

But since you only get one grand exit from this plane, it should probably be a good one. Like for me, I want to live a life that when I pass from and through this world, I want to leave a hole, one that gets filled with love and other shit. Stuff like the smell of cookies baking in the oven at Jimmy's house, and a fresh pack of 'ports, and Grandmaster Flash starting up at 140 decibels, and a hug and an ayyyyywhutsup from the whole fucking planet.

Do you know, somehow, when it's coming? Can you hone that sense, the way you can do with your intuition, the way you can get out of stuff if you just listen from your chest and somewhere in the center of your head? Or get into stuff, like when you can't lose at Hi Lo, betting the pot on a 5–10 turn, taking side bets from the watchers, doubling your money, taking everyone's loot? You don't get a ton of those moments, so don't waste them, but know when you're getting them. Sometimes you can spend them on other people.

I was sitting with JD in the Gold Coin Restaurant at Howard and Clark, picking at a tuna melt deluxe and a vanilla malt (best hangover cure ever), him at a coffee and cigarette, both of us telling lies. The Gold Coin was one of those diners in the city that appear about every eight blocks or so. Places like that all seemed decorated from the same 1950s scam plans foisted by guys named Chip and Mack on immigrant entrepreneurs and cooks who had saved up to buy out their white-flighted suburban owners. Brown wood-veneered booths with alarming orange vinyl padding, burnt-gold glass ashtrays, pudding-brown ceramic coffee cups, and an industrial shake mixer. A long, curved, sliver-specked Formica-topped counter lined with red pleather–covered stools leaking stuffing onto rarely swept floors. An obligatory cigarette machine by the front door and a bowl of stale buttermints on the counter. Andes and Ice Cube chocolate squares in foil for a nickel next to the cash register, the one with the heavy buttons and pop-up numbers that sits on top of a greasy-windowed display of kick-ass pies and cakes. Finally, the patrons provide a film of cigarette smoke that covers everyone and everything. At least the lights were incandescent. The whole place was staffed and patrolled and animated by waitresses in powder-pink uniforms with bleached white aprons, hennaed and blue-rinsed bouffants, and names like Flo, Jo, and Frannie. They chewed gum *and* smoked cigarettes while they worked. Virginia Slims and More menthols. Man, those Mores were terrible. But Tareytons were even worse, and those're what the cooks smoked while they took care of the food orders.

If you looked around before you went in, you could see how Clark St. turns into Chicago Ave. at the Evanston border, but the Northwestern train tracks and their attendant woods are running off to your left crossing both cities, and on their corner across the street over there is a big overgrown empty lot. It might as well have been a mountain pass to Transylvania or the last roll uphill before you dump into the ravine by Garryowen. It looked wild and wooly as fuck, a no-go no-man's land. We rarely crossed the border except on the El to go to Chandler's to try and steal stuff anyway, and we never crossed over at that corner on foot. I couldn't tell you why, even to this day.

I sat with my back against the wall, feet stuck out along the bench seat of the booth. Man, I needed some new shoes. These Chucks were ratty as fuck. Big toe coming through the top, the heel just hanging on, and the sides were starting to rip. I remembered JD and me were able to eat here because we just cracked some guy's piggy bank after we quick in and outted his crib after we watched him head out, to the liquor store we guessed. He came out the back door pretty fast and down the stairs. After he turned up the alley we ran up to his apartment and, sure enough, he didn't lock the door. We grabbed the ceramic pig (twelve dollars and thirty-nine cents in coins, two fives in paper), and I found a .25 under the couch cushions. I found a copy of Michener's *Tidewater* on the kitchen table. I stood there thumbing through it while JD made a Braunschweiger sandwich.

"Just don't tell me you need to take a shit," I said.

"Well, I might have to use the bathroom—"

"Oh no you don't. Keep it in your pants. That guy—"

"was drunk as shit, Teddy, c'mon, man."

"Yeah. But he didn't lock the door. He'll be right back. OP is only two blocks away."

"Fine. But I'm pouring a glass of milk," JD said.

"Alright. Wipe the mustard off your face and hurry up, jagoff." I walked over to the guy's TV and changed it from *I Dream of Jeannie* to some shit on PBS. Figured he didn't need any false hope.

"Fine."

JD finished that fat-ass sandwich in about twenty seconds.

Time to go.

"Alright. Let's hit it," I said.

"Yeah, yeah, yeah," he said, stuffing Stella d'Oros from the top of the fridge into his pocket.

"Fuck," I laughed at the grossness of those. "Don't you have *any* food at your house."

"You know we don't."

"Yeah. Sorry. Alright, *let's go*, motherfucker," I said from the doorway, the Michener going in the side pocket of my powder-blue cargo baggies.

"I'm coming."

"Alright then. Sko!"

We hustled down the stairs then turned left toward the street, headed through the gangway. As we turned right onto Damen, I looked over my shoulder and saw our man wobbling in from the alley, already chugging at a brick of Richard's. Shit, I thought. He won't miss a thing 'til tomorrow. I smacked JD in the back of the head maybe a little too hard, smiled big at his wide, wide white-boy eyes. He just stared at me, mouth twitching and unsure of itself.

We got to the head of the alley off the corner of Fargo and Damen and headed down toward Pottawattomie Park and its mess of open fields. I looked forward to getting there, needed some space. JD wasn't talking. I couldn't tell if it was because of the smack in the head, or the high off the score, or if the Braunschweiger wasn't agreeing with him, but I appreciated the silence, the fall air. Mid-morning Chicago in early October when everyone is at work and it's just you and the birds who haven't figured out it's time to head south yet? That shit is magic.

Once we hit the soccer/football fields, JD relaxed a little.

"I fount these in the bathroom," he said. He said "fount" like Frankie did. We got a weird mishmash of accents, truth.

"What the fuck are those?" I asked.

"10s."

"No shit. Valium. Dang," I said. "Gimme a couple."

He shook out three or four from the amber plastic bottle.

"Thanks," I said. "You can keep the rest," not feeling bad, but maybe a little generous. Besides, I don't really like downers, I'm waaaay more of an upper guy, if you know what I mean. But I could sell these, no problem.

"Thanks, Teddy," he said.

"Sure thing, Folks. No problem," I said. "Let's go eat something."

We headed across 3-D, the third baseball diamond. Hung a left behind the backstop and followed the fence line that marked off the tracks. Right before it gets to this person's backyard, there's a hole we widened and bent back in the metal chicken wire. We climbed through and headed up the side of the hill. We could've just walked another half block to the end of the dirt road and turned onto Birchwood, but the tracks are ours. We surveyed and walked it for that reason alone. This part of Chicago is weird. It's Rogers Park, a place incorporated by the city back in the day, one defined by Indian trails like Ridge Boulevard and Rogers Avenue. It has some tiny rural sections too, like this one behind the park. For those reasons alone, I dig it.

We walked the tracks for a bit, headed down the other side, and popped out behind the Clark station, next to Big Pit.

"Where we going, Teddy?"

"Gold Coin."

"You like that place, don't you?"

"Yeah, man. I like people waiting on me. And diners have everything on the menu. They'll make you whatever you want. And if it's owned by Greeks, they'll make it any time of the day. They made me a gyro omelet there once, no problem. It's pretty cool."

"Yeah. Okay."

"Let's split up the money now, okay?" I said. "While we're walking here."

"Sure," JD said, pulling all the coins out, squatting down and dumping them on the ground. He handed me a five and a shit ton of change. I'm good with it. I never told him about the .25, so whatever he hands me besides the paper is gravy, in my eyes.

He put the other five and the rest of the change in the right front pocket of his dark-blue baggies. It bounced around as he walked. Must've been a shitload of nickels and pennies. I laughed at this burgling penguin I'm walking around with.

"What's so funny?" he said.

"Nothing, man. All good. Let's go," I said.

We came out of the parking lot of Big Pit onto Clark Street. I saw Howard Street Bowl, its inscrutable windows probably hiding a bunch of Kings. We walked across the street from it until we got to Howard. Then we crossed over and headed into the Gold Coin.

The smoke and the fryer smell hit me full in the face as we made the second door after the little lobby with its pay phone. JD checked the coin return. Nothing.

"Two, sugar?"

"Yes ma'am," I replied.

"Right over here," she said. It's JoJo. She was cool, handled the more difficult customers. Had a three-pointed cross tattooed on one hand and a butterfly on the other. She put down two menus and a fresh ashtray.

"Coffees?"

"Yes ma'am," I said. "That'd be great."

"I'll be right back. Do you know what you want?"

"Tuna melt and a vanilla malt. How 'bout you, JD?"

"Just coffee," he said, hand on his stomach.

"Alright then. I'll just take these menus now."

"Thanks, Jo," I said, smiling over at JD.

She winked and walked off, writing a ticket for us.

"Them sandwiches finally caught up with you, huh?" I laughed.

"Fuck you, man," JD said.

"It's cool," I said. "But I'm gonna eat."

"Yeah. Whatever," JD said, lighting a smoke.

Jo came back with the coffee pot, filled us up, frowned at JD and his cigarette, drifted away.

I reached for the little silver creamer pot, JD grabbed the sugar shaker.

I slow stirred with a spoon, set it down on the saucer, lit a smoke. No sugar for me. I only had coffee with cream and sugar in it one time. After my ma kicked me out and I ended up living with my dad, we had coffee that first morning.

"What's for breakfast?" I asked him.

"Coffee," the old man said.

"Okay." I poured myself some into an old chipped piece of shit American Indian fundraiser memento he probably traded some cigarettes for and then added milk and a couple teaspoons of sugar.

"So you gonna drink it like a woman?" he said.

What the fuck, man. I haven't put sugar in my coffee since. It tastes just fine, but I still don't take it that way.

I glanced up at JD, dumping creamer in his coffee. He didn't look quite right. Sometimes, JD would get these moments of profound sadness written on his face. I wondered about that, how maybe it was his ma being a Latin Queen, or his sister being one too, but that he didn't know who his dad was, maybe that was it. All of us knew our dads, whether they had flown far or down the block to the bar. But not JD. It made his light a little dimmer sometimes, made him meaner, I think. I flicked my ashes on the floor under the table, too tired to reach over to the ashtray.

"What's up, Folks?" I asked.

"Nothin', Teddy."

"Alright. Be that way."

"What way?" he said, without looking at me.

"That way. You know what I mean."

"Ain't no *way* about it, man. Fuck you."

See what I mean?

"Never mind, Folks," I said, "'t's all good."

We sat in silence. JD stirring the shit out of his coffee.

"Knock it off, man. Just drink it already." I still hate the sound of clinky spoons in coffee cups. When I'm at home I even put the powdered creamer in the cup before the coffee just so I won't have to stir it.

"Fuck you. What do you care?"

See?

"Whatever, man. It's fucking annoying. That's all. Maybe you should pop a couple of those Valiums. Whatever."

"Whatever."

Jo brought my food. I'm about to tear it up.

"Can I have some of your fries?" he said.

"I thought you weren't hungry."

"Yeah, well. A little, maybe."

"Hold on," I said.

"Jo," I said, raising my voice a bit.

"What do you need, sweetie?" she said, coming back over to our booth.

"Can I get an extra plate, one of those little ones? I'm sorry. I should've asked you for it when I ordered," I said.

"That's no problem, baby. I'll be right back."

JD reached for a fry. I smacked his hand.

"I'm getting you a plate, fucker," I said. "Just hang on a second."

I really hate people touching my food, putting their hands near my plate, any of that shit.

Jo came back. "Here you go, hon," she said, setting a plate between me and JD.

"Thank you," I said.

"No worries. Anything else you need right now?"

"No. We're good. Thanks."

I followed her exit, and as I did I saw this guy sitting at the counter. He had a grey fedora sitting on the stool next to him along with his cigarettes, smoked Chesterfields. I recognized the pack, cause that was Grandma's brand. Vitalissed hair, red bumps on his neck from a super-close shave, especially around his Adam's Apple. Starchy white shirt, but shitty-ass shoes. Pretty rough, light-brown lace ups that had seen way better days. You can't front when it comes to shoes. Those are always the tell on a man. Check the shoes. I thought he was looking at us, but he was looking past us two booths back. At this family of towheads. Mom, smoking like a chimney, Dad, same, with a work shirt ("Mike") and greasy blue pants, two yowling white-haired kids, maybe four and six years old, a boy and a girl. Shit all over the table, napkins on the floor, lots of bouncing in the booth. Damn, I thought. Don't give your kids pop. What the fuck do you expect?

"Hey, Teddy. Remember that humbug with those Mexican Playboys at the bank parking lot?"

"What?" I asked, snapping back.

"That one where we were gonna move on those MPs and then

Big Taco showed up and shot that one kid?" JD said. "The one when the Grease helped us out?"

"Man what the *fuck* are you talking about?" I said.

"You know, Midget. That time with Giggs."

"You better quit with that shit," I said.

"Man, that shit was crazy, ennit?" he said.

"Motherfucker, you were like eight—you weren't even there!"

"Yeah, but when shit is legendary, it's like you were," he said. "Tell me the story."

"Nah," I said. "It's time to eat." I threw a handful of fries on the plate and pushed it JD's way. "Pass me that ketchup. I wish these fuckers would get that malt vinegar like they have at Arthur Treacher's."

We ate in silence for a while.

"What do you want to do after this?" JD finally said.

"I don't know, man. Why we always gotta be doing something?"

"I don't know. Fuck, man. Just asking."

"You finished eating?" I said, noticed the three or four fries on his plate.

"Yeah, I guess."

"No you ain't," I said. "Don't waste that shit." Sounded just like the old man, right there.

"Fine," he said, dunked the fries in my ketchup pile, popped them in his mouth.

"Goddamnit, JD," I glared at him.

"Sorry man," he laughed. "I forgot."

"It's fine," I said, drank some water.

The towhead kids behind us were starting to whine. I looked around for Jo or someone to shut them up, defaulting to expecting some mom to intervene. But it seemed that here, like my own life, was lacking that possibility. When I cut my eyes over to the waitress station, Grey Fedora was staring past us again. The kids whined even louder. Mom and Dad smoked, bitched about the size of the check.

I looked Grey Fedora up and down, winced at the shoes. They made me wonder a little more about him. The incongruity of the pressed shirt and the shit shoes, like he was trying to make his top half presentable, will folks to only look at his head and shoulders, never mind what was happening downstairs. That made me pause. And when he kept looking and writing in a Moleskine, I had to know what was up.

"I'ma go grab some mints. I'll be right back," I said.

"Okay," JD said, lighting a smoke. "Take your time."

"I will," I said.

I slow strolled up toward the counter. As I got to Grey Fedora, I stopped and pulled out my smokes, made a big to-do about pulling one out and lighting it. As I did, I looked over at his open journal.

Holy shit.

He had sketched out the towhead family. Mom, Dad smoking cigarettes, the kids, exaggerated kidly features like the big eyes and bashful faces; all were kinda crammed in the booth, in pretty accurate detail, and he had included himself.

And all their eyes were X'd out.

Their throats were all cut.

Charcoal-sketched blood pooled onto the table and down the sides of the booth he had drawn. And he was doing shit to the kids.

What the fuck.

I slowed a little, glanced at his face in passing, paused at his dead blue eyes. He was still watching them, his pigment-free gaze unwavering, unblinking.

I kept going, hit the counter. Grabbed a handful of mints, even used the scoop instead of my hand.

When I walked back, stuffing them all in my mouth at once, I stuck my elbow out, bumped him while he was staring over his cup of coffee. I could see right through his irises.

"Sorry, man," I mumbled.

He looked through me for a second, turned back to the tow-heads.

Jeezus.

I walked back to the booth.

"How about we hang out here for a minute?" I asked JD, slumping back into the booth.

"Did you bring me any?"

"Any what?" I said.

"Mints? Mints, fucker."

"No, man. No mints," I said.

"Fuck you," JD said.

See?

"You can get some on the way out," I said.

"Sure," he said. "How long are we gonna sit here, innyway?" That accent . . . he's starting to sound like an Indian.

"I don't know, man," I said. "I need to think for a minute."

What I thought about was this .25 in my jock.

"I gotta go to the can," I said.

"I ain't stopping you," JD said.

"I'll be right back," I said.

I went to the john, headed into a stall. I locked the door behind me, set my smoke on the toilet-paper dispenser and pulled up my shirt, grabbed the pistol. Checked the chamber (empty) and dropped the clip. Only five shells in there. Someone got shot, or someone got scared. That's okay. I'll take five out of six. I racked a shell, put the gun back in my waistband, flushed the toilet, and grabbed my smoke. Unlocked the stall and headed back out the door.

"You weren't gone long," JD said.

"You worried about me, Folks, need to know my piss habits?" I said.

"Nah. Just, whatever."

"Fine. Fuck you man," I said, probably amped up from fucking with the .25.

I finished my coffee, took a couple quick drags off my cigarette, and stubbed it out in the ashtray, closing one eye against the rising smoke.

"You alright, man?" JD said, looking over at me from his side of the booth.

"Yeah, I'm fine," I said, eyes wandering over to lock on Grey Fedora.

"Well you don't look fine. What the fuck are you thinking about?" JD asked.

"Nothing, man."

"Well shit, man. Maybe you should relax or something. I can feel the vibe coming off you."

"I'm good. Don't worry about it," I said. "Hey JD," I continued, "how would you feel about offing some Okie motherfucker?"

"I don't care. Whadda ya got?"

"There's a short-eyes fucker over at the counter. Grey fedora, peeping the booth behind us."

"No shit?"

"Yup. Have a look, but turn around slow, cause I wish this motherfucker would, but not in here."

JD slinked around, saw who I was talking about.

"Yup," he said. "You ain't kidding."

"You should see what he's drawing in that book of his."

"For real?"

"Yup."

"Let's do him. I hate assholes like that."

"What if he's your dad?" I said.

"Fuck you, Teddy."

I had that one coming.

"Alright," I said. "Let's do it."

I threw that five and a handful of change on the table, pushed it all in toward my plate on the wall side. Gotta keep people honest. I sat back in the booth one last time. Looked up again at Grey Fedora.

This time he looked back.

And not through me this time.

I stared at him for about ten seconds. Shot a quick glance back over my shoulder at the towheads, then back to him. And in that moment of recognition, my acknowledgement of who and what he was, of human eye contact, I knew I had probably saved a life or two.

But I wanted to make sure.

"Let's go, punk," I said.

"I'm ready, fucker," JD said.

As I scooched my way out of the booth, the .25 tipped up out of my pants and loudly onto the floor. I quick scooped it up, but in that splittest of seconds I knew. When I looked up, Grey Fedora had ghosted through the door, his stubby Chesterfield still burning in the ashtray.

At least not today, I thought.

Not today, you motherfucker.

19. BOY JOE

You from Mike Merlo's?

—CHARLES DEAN (DION) O'BANION

Me and Vassily, one day we take the El. I like riding the train. Vassily, he likes driving, but his limo is in the shop, getting an oil change plus detailed. I hope they clean the piss out of his car. The front seat is a fucking pigsty. I think we've talked about this before, but yeah. He's kind of a slob up there. So we hop on the Blue Line; he wants to head out to the airport, to O'Hare, see what everyone else is driving these days. Maybe that's what limo drivers do. I couldn't care less; I just want to get out of the neighborhood for a minute. I used to go to the airport when I was a kid, watch the planes take off. Man. That was so cool. Back then you could even walk onto the planes without a ticket. One time I was with some buddies. We walked around, went to the cockpit, were shooting the shit with the pilots, talking about flying and whatnot. After about ten minutes of talking and fucking with all these switches, one of them says,

"So hey. Going to Kansas City, huh? Do you have family there, or . . . ?"

"Holy shit," we say. "We ain't going to Kansas City."

The pilots laugh. "You are now," they say.

Dang.

"Hold on a minute," he says around the cockpit door. "Don't close that up yet. You better let these boys out. I guess they don't want to go to Kansas City."

"Hahahaha," he says. "Don't forget your wings."

But now, nah. You can't do that anymore. Shit. Can't do nothing no more. But still, it's okay to look around, see all the different people. Like the woman who knits her own hats. Who lives alone. Who's prepping for old and age and solitude. Cool people.

But you meet *all* kinds of people at airports. And sometimes coming or going to those airports.

Okay. Well maybe you don't meet them, maybe you're better off not meeting them, but you meet them in your heads, and well, yeah. You know you shouldn't meet them.

We met a couple of them. On our way home.

They got on the train at Belmont. I know that neighborhood.

So I'm looking at these two guys, occasionally in the face, but mostly their reflection in the glass. The one is pretty intense, and his eyes move around a lot. I'm pretty sure his name is Boy Joseph, full name only, and NEVER the initials. His buddy is Ned Lick—sounds like Nedly when you say it out loud.

This Boy Joseph cat's got red medium-length hair held back with sunglasses, like a manband, a guy's hairband; he's a forty-two-year old Irish gangbanger eating a sandwich, mouth wide open the whole time, bologna and miracle whip and shit coming out when he chews, black tank top, Black Panther leather jacket one or two sizes too big, a shitty version of Gary Oldman's Jackie from *State of Grace*, white-gold eyebrows and a red, red face, smugasfuck eyes looking at everyone on the train as his future victim. And if you peeled off that skanky tank top, you'd find that he's kind of guy who jerks off to the Nüremberg journals and has bathtub drain plug rings in his at-home nipple piercings.

Nedly is his crew-cutted duller-than-a-boiled-egg-fart sidekick with the low-key perpetually surprised face of a barely functional dipshit whose plodding approach to criminality is as rigid in its application as his sinister sometime-boss and all-time "best friend" Boy Joseph.

Vassily is kind of nodding off, dreaming of Ukrainian goat fucking or whatever, and doesn't see what's going down here, so I keep going, checking them out.

Boy Joseph and Nedly lost the benefits of their whiteness at about age twenty-three and then the longer prison stretches came. These two are up to more no good in one day on the outside than most people can imagine in their heads—drunk, high, or flat-out lunatic. I look close right quick when I see they're preoccupied with intimidating my fellow train lovers, starting to zero in on a victim, and looking at their eerie glow under the buzzy lighting I think white folks aren't pale, they're just continuously haunted . . . and for them, the fascination with Lestat and Hannibal Lecter, those cleaners, those refusers of freckles and the shallow and the subpar, reveal that haunting.

I'm not afraid of too much. Sometimes I think about things too much, like the conversation you have at that certain age; the one that connects old to young, when you have to decide which is worse, waking up in the casket under six feet of dirt or headfirst in the locked oven, the gas jets just turning up. Like that. But people? Not too much. I remember this one time I was working at Dreamerz and the Mentors played upstairs. My girlfriend at the time— who is *way* less afraid of people than I am—refused to wait on them, so they were more belligerent than usual. They finally came downstairs as I was closing up the bar. Because I am who I am, we were all getting along good, having some drinks and doing the white. I still had to close up though, so I was wiping down the tables after doing lines. I finished one and I looked up to see El Duce leaning over the bar to grab something out of the cooler.

I walked over, pulled a red cocktail straw out of the dispenser on the bar next to the napkins, and stuck it in his ass crack.

So, yeah. Not afraid of much.

I watch these two watching people. Well, okay, let's be real, it's Boy Joseph watching people and Nedly digging blackheads from his neck and smelling them. Boy Joseph's eyes light up when he spots, on this heretofore arrestingly dull day, a woman, Misty maybe, but really Ruth, or Lisa, who looks like a stripper on her day off trying hard to not look like a stripper on her day off. That she looks this way is not in any way an invitation to victimhood, but Boy Joseph and Nedly . . . don't care.

I believe they're answering in a very bad way the question I ask myself sometimes: Is life that full of sex and violence, or is it just full of the desire for sex and violence?

She knows it, knows that look Boy Joseph is giving her.

She looks up at the route map above the doors.

Next stop we're about to head underground, and I watch her calculate, say fuck it, and make to get off this goddamned train.

I nudge Vassily.

"Get up. We're getting off."

"Why doing this to poor Vassily?"

"Just trust me, man. We're getting off at the next stop."

"Fine, fine. But owe Vassily drink. Is this Polack neighborhood?"

"Shut it. Let's go."

If we get up now, it won't look like we're following Boy Joseph and Nedly, who I know are about to get off and pace this woman.

We stand at the doors at one end of the car; she stands at the other end.

Boy Joseph and Nedly get up, stand behind us. All I can smell is bologna and curdled miracle whip, white bread and rank vodka. Maybe even some Richard's.

When we hit the underground stretch, the lights kick on in the car and buzz back the reflection of Boy Joseph staring at my neck. Vassily senses what's happening, does what he does.

"Holy shit. Smell like some goddamn bologna here," he says.

Fuck. I try not to laugh.

"You're drunk," I say.

Boy Joseph runs his thumb and forefinger down the corners of his mouth.

Nedly farts, or has exhaled and needs to see a dentist.

The train stops and we get off.

"The doors are closing."

I slide my eyes over to the windows whipping by and watch Boy Joseph watch Misty.

She stops by a stanchion. Waiting for the next train, looks like.

Me and Vassily smoke cigarettes. Talk shit.

Boy Joseph and Nedly look at each other. Scheme. Try to figure out what's up.

One train goes by. People come and go.

She sits. Waits.

The platform clears out.

Boy Joseph and Nedly dart their eyes around. Nedly pisses off the platform, but never hits the third rail. Too bad.

They stare at her. Try to get her attention. Get bolder. Threaten her with their grimy white faces. Look over at us, but we just chill.

She gets up from the bench, walks over to the other side of the platform, looks down the tracks for the train, the one that goes to the airport. A white light comes screaming through the tunnel.

It stinks here. Like piss and alienation.

They walk around the maintenance room in the middle of the platform, come out the other side, make directly for Misty.

"BoyJoe" I say. This lank-haired fuck.

He turns, looks.

And just as the train comes in, she pushes back.

20. CEDAR

Again: I fear for the outcome of the Indian nations. Our people in their native state were not avaricious. They were on a common level; and, like the osprey that divides her last fish with her young, so they acted toward each other. But I find, to my sorrow, that, when you associate them with squaw men, and place them in power, they develop the wolfish greed of civilization, disregarding the rights of their less fortunate brothers.

—SIMON POKAGON, "THE FUTURE OF THE RED MAN"

"Teddy. Tell me a story but make it about me."

"JD, all the stories are about you."

"Not really. They're about you, man."

"They're about us."

"Fine. Gimme one. About *me*."

"I'll make you the star of one. How 'bout that?"

"Okay, fine den. But don't make me a cowboy, Injun. Or make me die like in that other one."

"Fine den."

Here we go.

The Montana blizzard was a standard. The rolling, cartwheeling prison bus was not.

Edgar had been drinking coffee and drifting through the white-out storm, lulled into that autopilot mode by the hyperspeeding streaks on all sides in the deep blackness, their high-contrast rushing around his view, creating a soft and silent world of inevitability.

Two brake lights winked way ahead of him, lost red eyes in the monochrome chaos that fluttered, stayed on strong, then suddenly whipped up eight feet in the air and leered at him as they sank over the side of the embankment, tracers in the open space between the road and the blue-white field of snow thirty-five feet below.

Even through the storm-dampened dark, he could hear screams and cries split the night wide open in ways that would never let it close for him the same again.

———

They had been bouncing through the late afternoon magic light and now night for what seemed like hours, even though they were in a bus, and on the road, and there were windows. Still, it was a prison transport.

And every second
was an hour
and every minute
was a day.

Tight, and cold, he passed the time blowing smoke rings with the vapor left in his cramped lungs. They pushed back, like the rest of his organs and everything else crammed down into the lowest profile possible, from his soul and his too-young face on down.

At least Montana was a little more casual, not like a transport in Chicago. They didn't have leg irons here. Shit, they weren't even chained to the seats. But they jammed everyone in there, some dudes three to a seat. The cuffs were on a little too tight, though. That, he supposed, was to make up for the rest of the small freedoms. He looked through the unbarred windows, past his fellow inmates. Out there were fading buttes, valley floors crusted in ice and shining crystal, cows, trains, and the smell of snow he couldn't quite catch in here.

Guys hacked and coughed, made small chitchat, talked shit. Scrounged through their bag lunches for scraps. Got up to take leaks, with permission, of course. A driver, three guards, and forty-four inmates including himself. He had joined them because of outstanding warrants from some bullshit case in Chicago. Did a burglary on some bro-house by Loyola University on the North Side. The judge gave him time served and he walked, but then the other three roommates pressed separate charges later on and warrants got issued. One crib—one felony he figured, so fuck that. But the law didn't see it that way. He heard about the warrants from Cesar, this one cop they used to get coke from every now and again. Ever buy blow off a cop? Some of the best shit you'll ever do.

JD thought about his current bullshit situation. How he got locked up. Some Montana Class A felony crap according to the Tribal cops. Him and Petey just fucking around, then Petey drunk as he'd ever get in his miserable life, deciding to hold up some shit liquor store in Billings. How he went along and then after how they boogied over to the Crow rez and promptly got ratted out by some asshole goody two shoes, probably a fancydancer, this bitch who lived on his girlfriend's couch. Tribal cops showed up at this chick's house on that grey and rainy afternoon, teardrops from the otherwise impassive iron sky the closest JD figured anyone would ever get to giving a shit about him. He smiled at the chick whose house it was as the cops dragged him to the squad car and she top-toothed it back to him. Now he was just pissed since the last female look he got came from a Crow girl, and well what the fuck. That and the outstanding warrants fucked him. Now here he was, because even though he wasn't Indian enough for enrollment he was too NDN for state prison, and more than enough Lakota for these Crow cops, so now he was on a bus. Getting transferred from the Tribal jail in Crow Agency to Crossroads in Shelby and then to some federal shithole lord knows where. Fuck.

He had finally resigned himself to do the time. Or so he thought. Cause now, looking back, he knew he wasn't ready. Shit, when all you own is time, you're never ready to part with it. He wondered if he got lucky, even as he tumbled through the air in this bus full of flying inmates and metal edges and screaming and blood and now some puke. Maybe being not ready was a way of praying, of letting Creator know that it wasn't going to work for you, that you needed help out of this situation, and that Creator Humor said, well I can't do that exactly, but I'll give you this.

And that's what he had to work with now. A flailing shitshow of howling guards and inmates, glass and viscera flying around him, time slowed to about twenty-four hundred frames per second and him fully aware of how much of it they had left, all while he moved at regular speed and worked to get his ass out of here, this single opportunity he figured for the once-in-a-lifetime shot he was going to get.

The Blackfeet guy that had given him tons of shit died when his big face pushed up into the ceiling as they flew through space. He could see his nose drive up into his brain, and he knew that was the end. The bus rolled in the air, and that dude came down grey. JD saw his chance. He twisted and dove for the guy's neck, got a hand on that and one under his chin, and then used his giant bucket-of-nickels head like a rock against the window, smashing it into the pane over and over again even as the bus lurched in flight, one of its back wheels catching the edge of a boulder on the side of the embankment as it arced over once more. The heavy glass diamonded and split, webbing finer and finer, catching light from somewhere up on the road, and then it began to drop away. He felt kind of bad using the guy's skull and whatnot to break the glass, but not that bad. Shiiiiit. Who was the asshole talking about Sioux this and Sioux that and making jokes about old-days captures and singing those weird White Dog songs? Not me, he thought. I'm just tryna eat a fucking sandwich and keep warm. This bitch had it coming. JD gave a final shove of that big Blackfeet cranium and out popped most of the window. Time slowed even more.

The ice-crystalled air rushed to fill his lungs, slamming into his teeth and nose as he worked to throw the Blackfeet down between the seats even as his feet pumped over his crumpling body to get to the gaping hole of light inside the dying bus. The screams rose and pressed in on his eardrums. He grabbed the sides of the broken window frame, glass shards digging unnoticed into his frantic palms as he launched himself into the blue and white quiet of the night, his body arching into the gravity-free space birthed by a sudden drop in the bus's roll, its front end catching the last rocky outcrop before the canyon floor rushed up to silence the men inside. JD twisted through space, landing prone on his back in a twelve-foot flat cedar, its fragrance embracing him as it broke his streak toward a rock pile five feet behind its moonlit shadow.

He breathed heavy, felt his chest and stomach for impalements, wiggled his fingers and toes and stretched his limbs, checking for breaks. Feeling nothing but the frozen air on his face, he reached deep in his left pocket, shackled hands digging for his cigarettes and lighter. He felt the branches under him, leaned his head way back, laughed, and lit a smoke.

———

"Ha, man. Nice."

"Does that work?"

"Yeah."

JD smiled, stared two thousand miles away, the safest place he could be.

21. UP YOURS, TOM WOLFE

I am now such and such years old. I have twenty-seven teeth. That's pretty good. My parents at this age, my stupefyingly terrible parents, they might've had sixteen teeth between them, and those were mostly molars, so I'm doing okay. This is not to say that they were bad people because they didn't have many teeth, but that they might not've had quite so many teeth as they could have because they weren't as nice of people as they could be, if that makes sense. Or if you subscribe to some sort of karmic dental charting.

My ma might still be alive. I don't know. We haven't talked in a lot of years, but no one's called me yet. She liked pills, smokes, whatnot, and since that catches up with you, who knows. My old man, though, he drank himself to death. There's really no other way to talk about it. His eyeballs, or maybe just the retinas, I think, were taken at his passing, put in some container somewhere to be used at a later date. That, I suppose, is one use of alcohol as a preservation tool. As the grandson of converted Catholics, he would give up beer during Lent and switch to vodka until the two-for-one filet o' fish went away. Said he "liked beer, so, yeah." That was his other sacrifice.

That was his commitment.

We used to talk when he was still around, when he moved out of the city, leaving Chicago for the land of his birth. We'd get together every couple weeks or so. On the phone. Which meant I would call him up at what used to be Grandma and Grandpa's place in Michigan (though he did call a couple of times in five or so years):

"How you doing, Pop?"

"Oh, pretty good."

Silence.

Silence.

Silence.

Silence.

"So Pop, had any good heart attacks lately?"

"Ha."

Silence.

Repeat.

But eventually we would talk about stuff. Slowly. Stuff not too deep. It became much easier for him after I had kids. That way he could ask about them, and that seemed to work for us.

One month I didn't hear from him. He didn't pick up when I called. I waited a couple months. Didn't know why in either instance. Then one Saturday:

"Hello?"

"Pop."

"Hey."

"Whatcha doin'?"

"Smoking a *fuck*ing cigarette."

"Where you been?"

"Jail."

"Oh. Okay."

Silence.

Repeat.

I mean really. Who the fuck goes to jail at sixty years of age?

My ma loved my pop. Pretty desperately, I thought. He loved her right back. I mean sure, when they got divorced, I was all, "Great! These assholes need to be *apart*," but they never shut up about each other after the divorce; would ask me questions about each other all the time.

Jesus. Just fucking call him, I would think, but say,

"I don't know" to her hillbilly face, already down a handful of teeth.

Pop never really talked unless he was shitfaced, so pretty much every night:

"Ah, Speedy. Your mother. Jesus. What a bitch. You know I loved her though, right?" he would whistle through his two missing bottom teeth, the second half of "Jesus" animated like a tired bird's sigh in the world.

"Right, Pop."

"I did, son."

"I know. I'm going to sleep."

"Okay . . . That bitch."

Jesus. Just fucking call her.

I think it was best he never did, though. Not just because he only could've when he was drunk and would have talked such corrosive shit, but because if he stayed sober, and they stayed together, he would've ruined her, ground her down, the way water does stone, his liquid existence laving away those edges, those angles and bends he first fell in love with.

This is another use of alcohol as a preservation tool.

On the other hand, he would usually come home so drunk that

he would just pass out. Thus, in those good old days, I never saw him punch *her* in the face.

This, too, is another use of alcohol as a preservation tool.

We drank together one night, and he told me things. Man. His childhood was destroyed by that one "friend of the family." So much pain. So much that could have been passed down.

And wasn't.

We drank a lot that night. Confessional drinking. Jesus probably leaned in at some point, called upon Creator, and said, "Pfffft. These two need'a go to bed." But he told me one thing I remember clear as a church bell.

He told me,

"I was a bad father. I'm sorry."

This might be the best use of alcohol as a preservation tool.

22. WE STILL CALL IT MAIZE

It was a crappy tin door, or maybe only an aluminum door, you know how tin foil is now aluminum foil, white and scratched, rusty and off at least one hinge, and it banged in the wind. Funny, I guessed, how that wind that was really the shit-stained endless breath of the citizenry sighing through this tired motherfucking town that hoped to grind me down from the looks in the grocery store to the sighs the old men gave me when they wouldn't even hire me to detassle their goddamn motherfucking corn. It banged and clanked and made me finally get out of bed, where I had been laying in the humidity and dust-swirled light, trying to make sense of the red-numbered digital clock on the floor next to the pile of dirty clothes with a sheet on top that he slept on, the clock that every time he looked at it, the one number would slip back, from 8:28 to 8:24, as if it was out there in the fire, off its leash, maybe checking out things it shouldn't be looking at, but this plane kept dragging it back.

I headed to the kitchen to make myself some breakfast, that door clanking at the edge of my hearing, but still.

Kinda weird,

I thought,

since I didn't usually eat breakfast.

Growing up in the city and heading to school having to cross Kings and Latin Eagles and Unknowns territory, it was better to eat something later in the day so you could keep your edge, and I had a hard time shaking that habit. Hanging out here in the sticks until things chilled back in the neighborhood, I thought maybe I could change.

I pulled the handle on the fridge, and the rubber door seal snapped and cracked like it hadn't been opened in three or four days. When I looked inside, I confirmed that no one had been in there for at least that long, because it contained a grimy glass bottle with a worn-off label and six drops of hot sauce at the bottom, some questionably dated generic mustard, and a packet of ketchup in the butter drawer. There should've been at least a grease-laden cardboard box with one or two curled and dried pieces of crappy non-Chicago midwestern pizza, but even that was out of the picture, so yeah, a few days at least. While this curated minimalism was painful evidence of my impoverished state, bonus, it helped out immensely with the kinda weird since I didn't usually eat breakfast department, and kept my streak alive, so kinda bonus. However, if I wanted to stay alive, I'd need some food or something, so off I went, hopping on my shitty bike, prepared to hook the chain back on at least twenty-eight times.

Today, Walmart smelled like farts and cancer. Visually, it wasn't all that different from other days when it smells like diabetes and piss stains, or cholera and shame, but today the scents were so downright arresting they clouded my eyesight and seemed to fog my shades. As I went to get my sorry-ass purchases recorded so I could load the receipt into the savings catcher app, I thought I'd found the source. They were at the checkout I just lined up for, but they were so fucking rotten all the other soul-crushed shoppers in this packed-as-shit-day-before-the-fourth-of-July-broken-airconditioned-store44-or-whatever-number-it-is were still going to stand in any line but this one. Lord have mercy. The son had two rows of teeth up top, Grandma was chugging a coke tallboy, and first daughter was all talkin' bout "when *I* fuckin go to Walmart, this is what it's gone be about."

Bingo.

The boy seemed just seventeen or so, his Travis Tritt shirt holey and handed down, his move to adulthood as awkward as his 'stache, wispy and wishful—*Someday I'll have pornstar status!* it thinks to itself as it looks around at its visibly countable numbers, all forty-five light-brown hairs barely hanging onto his upper lip. He couldn't see his shoes, but if he had some to begin with, they've probably worn away from his staring at them all the time, especially when Grandma yelled at him like she's doing right now. I watched the boy glance over at a rack with atlases lined up big and yellow, and I hoped this soon-to-be adult was thinking of the imagined terrains in maps; their ability to teleport him anywhere in the world would be his best friend right about now.

Grandma pulled the big red can away from her face for a second, breathed out heavy through her nose, her little lips lined right out to nothing. She had this hairdo that gave her the silhouette of an aroused harpy eagle; it worked well for her since it matched the constant terrifying look in her eye. Or at least I thought that's what Lurlene or Ashley or Tonya or whoever works at the closest Kut Above was saying and thinking when she gave it to her, thinking in between worrying that her scissors might slip, or that Grandma might get a chemical burn from the #46 Burgundy Apocalypse dye she insisted on getting, right before she murdered Lurlene or Ashley or Tonya or whoever at the closest Kut Above with a pair of her own shears, or a clipper, or a push broom, maybe.

Relax a little, would ya, Grandma?

I thought.

Your lips have pulled in on themselves and you look like one of those apple heads we used to bake when we were kids. I think your eyes are even falling in now, yeah?

Her deeply lined face told me I don't yet know that we don't really run away from things so much as we run toward things, their destructive and freeing natures not readily apparent at first but eventually loosing us from the bonds of polite society and other constraints on human desire. This woman has done things. To herself, and to others, but yup. She has done things beyond those bounds. Those things made her say things like,

"Are you fuckin' retarded?"

"What, Grandma?" said the son.

"I said, 'are you fuckin' retarded?'" she goes.

"I don't know what you mean, Grandma," he said.

"Jesus A Christ on the fuckin' cross, would you stop putting shit on the conveyor belt? The lady is trying to ring the shit up in the cart, dumbass."

"Oh. Sorry, Grandma."

"Not as sorry as your poor mother was," she charmed in reply.

Jeezus, Grandma,

I said to myself.

The cashier rolled her eyes and droned through her job, the dragging of almost out-of-date items across the scanner so tiresome, so draining and fatiguing that she wore a tiny battery-operated fan on a cord around her skin-tagged neck, its sad breeze blowing around her wispy curls and sour-milk sweat smell at the nominally frightened customers, their eyes a little wider at the prospect of that thinning hair getting tangled in the tiny motor and all kinds of hell potentially breaking loose. I went from chewing at my bottom lip to almost biting a hole in it so I don't sick it up here at the chip and jerky rack. My eyes watered a little, and my nostrils tried to close themselves up. I could only breathe out for so long, so I turned away and gulped air by the cold-pop cooler.

If vampires are god's fallen angels, then werewolves are his lapsed best friends. This I know to be true. This does not change. I have a handle on those two kinds of "monsters" for sure. But this Grandma, well, she's a for real monster, and I have neither a trite nor tight way to classify those. Humans make the worst monsters; they're rent souls who parlay in the iciest of truths. I want to imagine what's happened to this woman to make her so hate the tendons that hold the world and its people together, what makes her want to rip and tear the flesh from the webbing of the living, but I can't. I can only add it to the list of questions I try to remember to ask myself when I'm on the crapper or smoking outside the hayseed bar in the town square, the Ritz, or the Waldorf, or whatever hi-tone rich-people mask it wryly wears.

I put the chain back on for the twenty-ninth time (tough day) just as I was rounding the corner back to the dump I called home, a "Bless This Mess" sampler picked from the alley waiting to mock my arrival and remind me to work harder or something. I set my very warm ham and cheese loaf (luxury purchase, but I refused to eat bologna), liquefying mayo, and generic white bread down on the hot-as-fuck sidewalk and fixed my goddamn bike, deciding to walk the last couple hundred feet rather than make it thirty.

I freed a hand to grab the knob and push open the unlocked door (why bother?), then threw the bag, the bike, and myself at the gold plaid couch just inside the entryway to Satan's personal shitter. Sweat rolled. Beams creaked. Nails popped. Flies buzzed.

I passed out.

When I finally woke, I rolled over and away from the cushion full of a thousand dead farts and felt the fine alligator lines of the itchy nylon couch threads pressed into my face. My shorts were jacked up my ass; my sleeveless T-shirt was twisted around my neck and under my sleep-induced dead right arm that sort of flopped at my side like a frog with a fresh pin in it. I shook off the buzz of awakening nerves and walked into the kitchen with my purchases straining against the cheap plastic bag that had recently held my sleeping foot.

I made a sandwich (two meats, one bread; folded up with a blob of mayo). Drank some water from the tap. Ate six OTC liquid pain pills, brushed my teeth with my finger (because colder water after, not because hygiene), and put on a fresh T-shirt. Went back to my finely furnished living/dining/bedroom and read a shit ton of Patricia Highsmith.

Sweat rolled. Beams creaked. Nails popped. Flies buzzed.

Shortly after Ripley forged some more paintings, I decided to look out the front window, hoping I'd see Florence, or Capri, or at least fucking Naples.

No such luck. But it did look a lot like Haddonfield in magic light, so there was that. The piano riff played in my head as I headed into the kitchen, its rear wall full of dusty glass and cracked wood window frames, the ghosts of curtain rods framed in dirt and little nail holes, some spectral prairie marm weeping from the other side at the thought of moldy red and blue gingham.

I looked out the back window, expecting to see nothing, a reflection of this town and what my life had become lately. Even so, railroad tracks and corn rose up into my view.

Corn.

And corn.

Still and brooding.

It finally got dark. I headed up town, sweating less, cussing more.

Guess I'll bounce a check at the pizza place,

I thought.

I took the small cheese pizza that I overwrote a fifty-dollar check for, brought it to the bar, and handed it out to the farmers gathered around the TV in the back, pouring salt into their pilsner glasses of Old Milwaukee.

Then I'd play them Jeopardy for money.

And never lose.

There was no need to hustle. These guys would get so pissed at me, they were happy to double or nothing again and again. They were nothing like the morning crew, the guys I'd bet I could do the NYT crossword in fifteen minutes or less, the ones who were crabby, less drunk, and a whole lot cheaper than these dudes on the night crew, who were happy to be out of the ten-thousand-degree fields.

"What is Aroostook County, Maine?" I boomed across the bar, seeing the "The site of a bloodless 1838–1839 war between Britain and the US" flash across the screen. When the contestants had all fucked it up, I even got to mock always-pedantic Frenchy Trebeck's shitty mispronunciation of "Aroostook."

Everyone laughed. Well, except for the waitress (who hated my guts) and two cats playing pool in the side room, but they probably didn't hear, seemed pretty drunk anyway.

I managed to get two or three five-dollar bets that I could run the table. Business was slow tonight. I couldn't believe it with the way the heat was. Well

let's go, rednecks,

I said, under my breath.

I knocked out the first round no problem, collected my money, and even bought back sixty-cent drafts for each of these cornpone cracker fucks. Drank two Jim Beams and three drafts of my own. Life was okay. But it was time for Double Jeopardy. A couple of the now-drunk farmers went for ten-dollar bets, and the two pool sharks ambled over, asked to get in.

I thought,

What the hell?

They sat a ways away, held their highball glasses close.

"Films of the '80s for four hundred, Alex."

"This 1981 John Landis film featured an English pub named 'The Slaughtered Lamb.'"

"What is . . ."

I laughed.

Seriously?

For fuck's sake.

The round dragged on. "The Ottoman Empire." "Who is Attaturk?" "What is 'The Old Man of Europe?'" blahblahblah.

"Medieval Murderers for one thousand, Alex." My ears pricked up.

I made a quick side bet with the bartender for twenty bucks that I could answer before the clue came up. The big man took the bait.

"Who is Gilles de Rais?" I quickly said.

The bartender looked over at the screen—

"This fifteenth-century French nobleman ultimately confessed to the killing of dozens of children . . ."

—and balled up the twenty in his hand, threw it over the bar at me.

Who's next, I thought.

Vlad Tepes?

Jesus Christ. This is weak, but weird.

I didn't like where this was going, looked at the two dudes at the end of the bar. Seriously? I laughed. Probably too loud. But you know. There's no way. Besides, they *both* had tans.

WhowWhowWhow!

"The Daily Double."

"I'll take 'Sixties Shows' for two thousand dollars, Alex."

The answer flashed as I hopped off my barstool.

"The ce-ment pond, motherfuckers!" I yelled on his way to the bathroom, thinking,

Everyone knows where Granny washed the Beverly Hillbillies' clothes.

When I came out of the can, they were waiting for me, doing lines off the backs of their hands and leaning next to the door, which stood at the head of the long hallway, near the end of the bar. They blocked my return to that wood-sided, cigarette-burned salvation and slowly edged me out the back door, the bartender's profile against the TV light already fading from my vision.

And I knew

this was it. How fucking ignominious, Alex,

I thought.

Bugs whirred. Sodium arc lights buzzed. Car windows sweated. Thunders boomed.

God's fallen angel held my arms while god's lapsed best friend punched me in the sternum. Six times.

The seventh hit drove a rib through my heart. I fell to the ground, thinking,

Please don't let my arms spread out at my sides.

I fucking hate clichés.

The corn rustled.

23. TEST PATTERN

It was my second call from a dead person in a week, wtf. This one was a Fishman or something, something with an old lady first name . . . Bernice? Or Flatula, Begonia, Garnet. Maybe Hypatia. Fuck. I can't remember. But just like the other, as soon as I Googled her number, sure enough . . . this one, d. 1989. Shit. I hate talking to dead people. Especially when I've been taking a nap. We're supposed to be the suicide hotline team, fielding calls from prospective customers, but sometimes business gets slow. And once in a while, old clients remember our number. It's a second gig I've had to take since the night job lost its rowdy appeal.

This is no bullshit you find out at the end I'm a ghost kind of story. I'm fucking dead right now. We can get that out of the way. I sit on your couch and watch you live your life, hope that you pick a good movie, make some goddamn pizza rolls or something. Because I can see, I can hear, I can smell, but I can't feel—well, okay, I got feelings, but I can't feel in the physical way, so you better fill up those other senses, John Denver style, or it's the chains and the moans for you and yours.

Actually that part *is* bullshit. They don't let us do that anymore.

Some kind of big meeting a couple years back. God, Luscious Beelzebubba and his crew, the Magdalene, the Nazarene, the Archangel Michael, Iblis, Baby Jesus, Teen Jesus, the djinni, Moses, the rusul, some dusty Pharisees, Peter, Paul, and Thomas—no Mary—basically *all those people* got together and put the kibosh on the whole fun haunting thing. It's a total load of crap, if you ask me. Yeah, I'm a royal fuckup, and so it's the *wanagi* life for me—just a ghost, still a Lakota (awesome), but not a cool spirit, not moving on, nope, and so we don't have much out here to do. When you're a *wanagi*, you're always looking for a little something to eat and kinda hanging around. It's hard to get people's attention, you know. Before the meeting I could ride a horse, throw rocks, pass gas, booo-oooo-ooo it up, but now, nothing. The order came across the one goddamn TV station we have out here. You remember in the old days when the "Star-Spangled Banner" would play, and then Indian Head, and then good night and *ccckkkkraaackkkkcrrrrackkk* static and bug races? Ever wonder what happened to that? Yup. It's us. That's *our* TV station now. It's all that's on on this side of the veil. The thousand-mile-an-hour pixels flying by are all the cool souls that are moving on, and we have to watch them go. And if they need to get us any info, they loop a crawl across the bottom that looks like the graphics from the first Pong game ever invented.

That day bhoots, pretas, yurei, nu gui and ba jiao gui, Cho-Nyo-Gwishin, abambo, kehua, muldjewangk, my good buddies wana'ri, nésemoo'o, biitei, nanaikoan, cipay, and sometimes even ch'įįdii (hah, *jokes*, my Diné cousins), all looked up in dismay at this total bullshit directive creeping across the bottom of the screen:

From this day hence [so pompous—who the fuck talks like that?], *all manner of haunting shall be limited to shadowing the living in a spirit of love and friendship. There shalt be no wailing, clanking of chains, wringing of skeletal hands, clacking of teeth, wearing of sheets, tossing of furniture, chilling of air, snuffing of candles, nay, nor indeed any other action that might alert the quick to the presence of the dead.*

Yours truly,
Father, Son, Holy Ghost, et al

Like I said. Total bullshit.

We tried to organize, get together, pull a no-Western-traditions demand to be heard, but it was like trying to get into a literature conference as a unified group. Too threatening, too cutting edge in our haunty ways, we were a threat to the spectral status quo, and so the memos. Since we refused to fragment by area and ethnicity, we were doomed, stuck with these crappy fake-nice directives and these vaguely threatening calls from long dead Naperville house-wives and Long Island matrons, Simi Valley Vicodin ODs and deader-than-doornails Orange County closet coke fiends.

What did we do?

Well, shit. There's nothing we can do. Resigned to our fates, we haunt the dreams of indie filmmakers, taking our repressed ideas out on their minds. They become our voices, our vehicles to speak the words of America's oppressed and forgotten dead.

And we'll never let them go.

See you at the awards shows.

Afterworlds

P.S.—Just so you know, the other side is just like this side, but with a couple cool extra things. There's still gangbanging and all, but here you don't die *and* you're a lot closer to some other sides, so weird stuff can happen, like this time when

we talked a ton of shit one summer night, when the air outside was soft and the light was so warm you could sleep on the sidewalk just forever. Ten or two or four immortal teenagers with an endless supply of icy beer in sweaty brown bottles we chugged and threw over our shoulders into the street when we were done drinking and had finished burping. We sat along the guardrail on Fargo Ave. at Pottawatomie Park that kept drunks from driving off into the football field / baseball diamond / soccer field because the street was a perfect ninety degrees and the city must've figured it was cheaper to put up a long, corrugated piece of metal than to replace the streetlights we kept knocking out and the sign we kept taking down because, well, that shit is funny.

The dark rippled and rolled under Chicago's own North Side brand of visible humidity, and our voices pressed back down into our own faces, the night's fog keeping our noise and our boombox sounds out of the homes of anyone who would've called the cops. You know, one of those perfect deep summer nights, yellowy arc light carried on a breeze that's just enough to keep you from getting too hot but not too much that you have to put your shirt on, cover up that new needle, string, and India ink The Cross is Boss tattoo you did the other night, the one that might be infected but still looks cool. A perfect listless Tuesday that you remember one afternoon cutting through the lines of minivans and tired SUVs in some soul-crushing parking lot on your way to get keys made, or a flat of petunias, or some bullshit like that. A night just damp enough that all the fireflies in the city decided they needed to get laid and came over to dance in that field so currently free of drunks and drivers and any activity but collecting dew. Jimmy and JD talked shit like they usually did, spit the laws of Folks and the six-pointed star, LoveLifeLoyaltyKnowledgeWisdomandUnderstanding, not because they cared but because they needed each other to help them remember all that shit and then remembered how proud they were to be Royals and not BGDs, Ain't No Pity in Simon City, how brave they were, how much they hated Kings, made fun of each other's moms, and then slowly noticed the fireflies starring all around their heads, like they had ascended to the heavens with no celestial warning. Jimmy was always smarter, and quicker, and he flung his half-full beer and caught a handful and smashed the lightning bug butts onto the ends of his thumb and pointer and pinky fingers so he could make an upside-down crown in the dark, King Killer, but JD just rubbed them on his teeth and grinned and made us laugh, his always-toxic mouth now appropriately adorned in glowing greeny-yellow.

It flowed through the alleys like a waterless flood, rose up the sides of broken-brick garages, hissed along bleached yellow-sided sheds, and silently drowned the sumacs and chicory that grip the blacktop like ghost-colored two- and three-leafed urban bonsai. It was the breeze that blew through the midsummer dark, pulled at the veil between the worlds that's oh-so-thin right now. Balances and harmonies teetered so delicately and sometimes came down just a little bit *wrong*, their landings bringing the unexpected through the caul into the world on our side. We sensed a shift in the air, cooler than before, but as we blinked through this new fog it wasn't why we shuddered.

The now twelve-foot-tall lightning bugs snapped at us; their fuzzy pincers and spiky arms held us at the throat and pulled steadily down with their third and fourth legs until we just popped in their hard, unyielding embrace, and they smeared our blood on their forelegs and draped our intestines between their antennae and chittered, eyes flashing, their abdomens glowing brighter in humor and health, as they skittered through the dew in that cold, green field, the one no drunks will dare for a long time to come, our failing cries sunk into the grass out of sound, and then sight.

I watched JD's smile fade in the dark.

Acknowledgments

Chicago ✶✶✶✶, my city, my rez. I miss you every day. The almighty mighty 𝕹𝔬𝔯𝔱𝔥 𝔖𝔦𝔡𝔢. Uptown, BoysTown, Downtown, Rogers Park. Amie, who tried me to get me to write these stories for years. Emily, and Max of course. All the readers of *Sacred Smokes*, and all the editors at the magazines and lit journals that published early versions of some of the work in this book: *Yellow Medicine Review, Red Ink: International Journal of Indigenous Literature, Art & Humanities, Unnerving Magazine, Red Earth Review, Mad Scientist Journal, Literary Orphans, Open: Journal of Arts & Letters,* the *Journal of Working-Class Studies,* and the *Massachusetts Review* for popping off with the opening chapter. NALS (Native American Literature Symposium) and all the Clan Mothers and Brothers who got the first taste in a visual way of what this book was going to look and sound like, John Gamber and Fantasia Painter, David Stirrup, David Carlson, Scott Andrews, Brother Billy Stratton. The Working-Class Studies Association, Tillie Olsen, Bill Hillman, Tony Bowers, The Rt. Rev. Martin Billheimer, Rev. Jack and Rexella Van Impe, D♞B♞H. ♘ Cholera Ranch ♟. Miss Sally Timms, Kenneth Morrison, the many many who supported *Sacred Smokes,* now in its second printing, and Portland State University for giving me some time to go out and get it there. Rebecca Lush, Anita Comeau at Prairie Edge, Dorene Wiese, JoAnn Maney and all the Uptown folks and the rest of the Native community in Chicago, Mark Turcotte, Boone Sings in the Timber, Book Cellar, City Lit, Co-Prosperity

Sphere, the Chicago Public Library and their seven copies of *Sacred Smokes* along with all the libraries who put the book on their shelves—there's more than a hundred of you at last count—El Milagro, Chicago diners, theaters, and bookstores, Ray Rice and my alma mater the University of Maine at Presque Isle, Kathleen Rooney at the Chicago Tribune, Bill Savage and his Chicago Reader review, Voices in the North Country, Libra Distinguished Lecture Series, Gabino fuckin' Iglesias—thanks for the support and for supporting so many. We appreciate you. Kesean Coleman, thanks for all the support and for hooking us up in Portland. Miss you, young brother. Central New Mexico College and Brian K. Hudson, Lee Francis and Red Planet, Montana Book Festival, Portland Book Festival, Susan Bernardin, Oregon State University, Institute of American Indian Arts, Santa Fe, New Mexico, AWP 2019, Janice Lee, Brian Twenter and the students at the University of Minnesota, Morris, the Portland State University Creative Writing Program Reading Series, all the readers and listeners at Woodland Pattern, Milwaukee, Wisconsin, the University of Colorado, Boulder, Utah State University (and the folks at Access Utah / UPR), California State University, San Marcos, California State University, San Bernardino, Multnomah County Central Library. California State University, Northridge. And hey, Los Angeles, second biggest market for *Sacred Smokes*. I knew you loved me back. Laura Furlan, Toni Jensen, Eddie Generous, Jeanetta Calhoun Mish, Ho-Chunk Nation Chicago Branch Office. Ito Romo, thanks for all your support and your own words and work. Everyone else I'm sure I missed here, sorry about that. Colville Business Council Chair Michael Marchand, who said, "Wherever the Creator put us, we think that's where we should be."

Stephen Graham Jones. I can never thank you enough for your generosity. I owe you a burrito, I think.

Mona Susan Power for so very much, always.

Elise McHugh. Thank you.

Stephen Hull, Bryce Emley, Felicia Cedillos, Katherine White, and all the good folks at the University of New Mexico Press. And a tip of the hat to James Ayers, a copyeditor extraordinaire who should write my blurbs. Thanks for getting what I'm doing on the page.

Sister Stacy Two Lance, brother Chris Brooks, the whole Hehaka Oyate—love and compassion always. We hope we're being good ancestors.

All the boyz and girlz who are gone but never forgotten. I miss you being in this world.

Is it more of the same? Well, kinda. There're so many stories and folks kept asking for more. A young man from Philly dm'd me one night on Instagram and asked when the next ones were coming. That's when I decided to tell them. But I wanted to show the maturation of the teller, the technique and structures reflecting his growth and aging. I'm hopeful I did that this time out, cause like Miles Davis said, "Man, sometimes it takes you a long time to sound like yourself."

Finally, as always, the ancestors. We hope we're all you thought we'd be.